The Missing Maid

by

Morgan W. Silver

This is a work of fiction. Similarities to real people, places, or events are entirely coincidental.

THE MISSING MAID

First edition. September 30, 2021.

Copyright © 2021 Morgan W. Silver.

Written by Morgan W. Silver.

Also by Morgan W. Silver

Maggie's Murder Mysteries
Prelude to Poison
Poised to Quill
Booked For Murder

Maid for Murder
The Missing Maid

Monday Moody
The Chrono Unit
Unparalleled Affairs

Standalone
The Exciting Life of a Minor Character

Watch for more at www.authormw.com.

Chapter One
The Sheep Did It

Greystone in Surrey was a cute village with wonderful amenities. There was a spa, several yoga retreats, dozens of psychologists who all drove BMWs, and plenty of lawyers who played golf. The village was surrounded by green paddocks and the occasional dairy farm, as well as large estates with gorgeous Georgian homes. It was the perfect place to con wealthy snobs.

And that was why I was here. My real name's... not important. I came here with the name of Clara McIntyre, which I considered a perfectly innocent name and fitted the persona I had adopted for my con. It was a long one; I would have to be patient.

I had done my research and mixed with a dose of luck, I found a place I could rent relatively cheap. The main reason the flat didn't cost much was because it was above a pub called The Drunk Sheep. At least it looked better than it sounded.

I had brought one suitcase and a backpack and stood there observing the building. It had a black exterior with golden letters and several potted plants with ivy draped over the edges to make it look cosier. There were two picnic tables outside, but it was only eight in the morning and the pub wasn't open yet. I imagined people would use them if they opened since the weather was still nice. It was August and it would only get colder from here on out.

My landlady was also the owner of the pub, and I'd only gotten the name Agnes. I tried Googling her and the pub, but nothing came up. I didn't like knowing so little about who was going to be renting me this place. Information was power.

Which is why my name would result in nothing but the latest pictures I had added to my new Facebook account, just in case someone would look me up. I had a very realistic-looking ID card with a picture of me with my newly coloured auburn hair, and it didn't matter what my backstory was; nobody would be getting much out of me. Also, I had serious doubts anyone would care. I'd keep to myself, and my wealthy clients wouldn't be chatting with me much.

I looked for the side entrance and entered a narrow alley. The building on my left was a small bookshop. I made a mental note to visit it sometime. My mother had always made Sundays reading days, and I missed spending a whole day reading.

Despite everything, I missed her.

The alley had a couple of bins but nothing else. It led to another cobbled street. It would be beautiful to take strolls around this place, I imagined.

I knocked on the door and waited. This would be my first interaction as Clara McIntyre, but I was ready.

The door opened and before me stood a woman in her late fifties with short, grey, curly hair that looked like it hadn't been combed since the seventies. She had a plump figure and two different coloured eyes, one brown and one blue.

It was a condition known as heterochromia, which I was planning on blurting out in my enthusiasm—my aunt had it as well—but I was distracted by the ripped fabric of her black shirt and the bewildered look in her eyes.

"I'm Clara," I said. "You must be Agnes."

"Hurry inside. I can't leave her alone with the havoc she wreaked," she said, and pulled me into the small corridor. There was a staircase to my left, and broad double doors behind Agnes. They probably led to the pub.

She hurried past the staircase and we entered a long and narrow kitchen that smelt like chicken soup. It looked cluttered and like it was used well. It made me smile. I wasn't exactly a kitchen princess.

We went into the garden.

I figured we had passed her private kitchen and that the small garden was also only accessible to her. It was fenced off and there was a door in it, probably so she could move easily between here and the pub garden. It would be so noisy here at night. Good thing I had brought earplugs.

I turned my attention to the centre of the garden and gaped at the scene before me.

"The garden isn't usually like this," she said. "But Betty is."

"And that is the name of the black sheep?"

She nodded.

"Who is eating the laundry from your clothes line."

"Yep. She's got a binge-eating disorder."

The black sheep was currently munching on a purple bra and half of the clothes line had been taken down.

"I see," I said.

"And she's clumsy."

"Clumsy?"

"Yes. She's always causing accidents." She turned to me and smiled. "You'll see."

What had I walked into? "Should I be worried?"

"No." She still had that smile on. It was becoming eerie now.

"If I get murdered in my sleep, I will haunt you," I said.

She blinked at me, then laughed. "I had a good feeling about you, and turns out I'm right. Come on, help me with Betty and I'll show you to your new abode."

"Alright," I said and advanced. I grabbed one end of the bra and started pulling.

Betty remained in place and was surprisingly strong. Agnes's idea of help was telling Betty to let go.

I stopped pulling and opened my mouth to tell Agnes to try something else when the sheep suddenly pulled her head down and yanked me forward. I fell flat on the ground.

"Okay. Do you have an assault rifle? Because that seems to be the only thing that can stop her; she is really dedicated to eating clothes." I got up and dusted off my knees.

"Yes, she'll eat anything. It's like she has an iron stomach. Unfortunately, I left my assault rifle in my other trousers, so we'll have to make do without." She shook her head as we approached the black sheep. "And just as I was in the middle of cooking. I heard that Misty's husband cheated on her, so I'm making her favourite soup. There is nothing that my cooking can't fix."

Except her husband's wandering eye. On the topic of wandering eyes, mine were still on Betty who had now consumed an entire bra and two shirts.

"Isn't this bad for the sheep?" I asked.

"She once ate a bunch of bolts, three lemon pies, and a straw hat. This is nothing."

We bent down and hurriedly picked up all the clothes. Betty moved towards me as soon as she stopped chewing.

"Does she eat humans?" I asked with a grin.

"Ha," Agnes said, but then stopped and frowned as she considered this.

Great.

Agnes laughed when she saw my concern and then took Betty by the pink collar she had around her neck. She directed her back to the corner of the garden where she had some peaches.

Betty attempted one more bite out of Agnes's shirt but after a stern talking-to, she finally focussed on the peaches. I guess she did listen to Agnes.

I brought the clothes into the kitchen and placed them on the wooden breakfast table. The kitchen was actually not bad and had a decent fridge and some nice cabinets, but it hadn't been cleaned in at least two weeks. There was dust, some smudges here and there and some dried up dirt near the entrance. My hands were itching to clean.

Agnes closed the door to the garden behind her. "Thanks for your help. Follow me to your new flat. It's small but has everything you need. The space upstairs is divided into two flats with separate entrances to both. You won't see your neighbour much, except for in the pub. Or if you decide to take yoga. Pavani has her own yoga studio." She glanced back over her shoulder. "She's in her eighties, but she can fold herself up like an origami bird."

I smiled at that image as we headed up the stairs. The steps had recently been hoovered and it seemed that Agnes had done her best to make things nice in order for my arrival. That gave me a good feeling, at least. Then again, I would probably clean everything from top to bottom as soon as she left me to settle in.

Transforming something from dirty to clean gave me a great sense of accomplishment. I didn't have control over a lot of things, but at least I could control that.

There was a small landing where we stopped so Agnes could unlock the door. Attached to the key was a key chain of a black sheep.

I grinned.

We stepped into a small square hallway where I left my suit-case and backpack. The living room was cute. There was a yellow sofa with one blue cushion, as well as a nicely sized TV. A fireplace was placed in the corner with an armchair and poof. The kitchen was behind the living room, separated by a half wall so I could see right into the kitchen. I liked that.

There were large windows with flowery curtains. My view wasn't that great since I faced a building similar to this one. It had the same large windows but I couldn't see through them due to the blinds.

Agnes showed me to the final room: the bedroom with adjoining bathroom. There was also a walk-in closet. The space in this flat was used well, so it was more than enough for one person. Besides, I was used to small living spaces. I had always lived in tiny flats. This, however, was a nice size.

My bedroom had a French balcony, and I opened the doors. The flat opposite me also had a French balcony right across from mine. They probably mirrored the lay-out of this place. I looked down into the narrow alley that separated us.

"Harry runs the bookshop next door and also rents out the place above it. When I came up with the idea of turning the upstairs place into flats, he showed me his. Since my building is bigger than his I was able to change the first floor into two flats, whereas he only has the one. His flat is still pretty much similar in lay-out. Though mine are way more stylish," she said with a wink.

I looked around the room with the colourful splashes and quality furniture. "I don't doubt that for a second."

She beamed. "I'm glad you like it. I did my best to make it nice."

"I can tell," I said. "And where are you staying?" I couldn't imagine her living far from her pub. Or Betty.

"I live in the basement. I'll show it to you whenever you want."

"Well, thank you. I appreciate your help."

"You're welcome. You said you were staying for a few months, right?"

"Yes. Just to see if I can get enough work here as a maid."

"You said that, yes. You're good at cleaning, huh? That's good to know. You might be able to hand out some good tips."

Before I could respond, she said: "Where are you from?"

"I've moved around. I've pretty much been all over England. Mostly cities." It made it easier to steal and con.

"Why move around so much?"

"My mother's job," I said.

"Oh, what did she do?"

I gave her a smile. "If you don't mind, I'm tired and I have lots of things to do in order to get settled."

She nodded. "Okay. Thanks for braving Betty with me, and let me know when you want a tour of the pub." She placed a hand on my shoulder. "This place is like a warm blanket. You'll enjoy it here."

I narrowed my eyes at her. Why tell me that? Perhaps I wasn't as good as I thought about hiding the sadness I carried around with me. I touched the ring on my right hand.

It had belonged to my mother's mother. No matter how bad things became, my mum would never sell that ring. Even if it was worth over five thousand pounds.

She gave it to me the last time I saw her.

I sighed and realised Agnes was still there. "Thanks," I said, hoping the pain wasn't too visible.

She squeezed my shoulder and then left. I waited until I heard the door close.

I walked around the flat. This would be my life for the next few months. I'd be fine as long as I stayed focussed. I had a goal, a mission. And I had to succeed.

My small suitcase contained very few personal effects. I simply didn't have many. We had moved around too much for me to have collected anything. I had an e-reader because physical copies of books just weren't practical, I had my phone on which I stored pictures and played music, which left my cleaning supplies and clothes. That was pretty much it. The ring was the only sentimental thing I had.

I used a self-made all-purpose cleaner to wipe all the surfaces and then hoovered the floor with the hoover I found in a closet next to the kitchen. I then sprinkled baking soda on the sofa and let it sit for half an hour before hoovering it.

Next, I cleaned the bathroom with my spray filled with vinegar, baking soda, and dish soap. I also cleaned the toilet and sink and then took a shower. The next thing on my to-do list was my first cleaning session at my first client's house. So far, she was also my only client, but hopefully that would soon change.

I still had an hour, so I might as well check out the pub and maybe wander around a bit.

Agnes was in her kitchen. I wasn't sure what she was making, but it smelt like vanilla now.

"Hey," I said.

"Oh, there you are. I've been making something for you. It's a flan. My special recipe. It always cheers people right up. I've just finished."

I figured I wouldn't ask her why she thought I needed cheering up. I really needed to work on my poker face. My mother always taught me that it didn't matter what my personal feelings were, I had to hide them behind a mask and show people what they wanted to see. It depended on the con what that was. Right now, I was supposed to be a quiet cleaning lady. There would be no more slips.

Agnes handed me a plate with flan and blueberries on the side. I jiggled it and smiled to myself.

"I do that too," Agnes said. "It's my favourite part of eating the flan."

I took a bite and closed my eyes. A moan escaped and I looked up at Agnes. "This is amazing," I said.

She blushed. "Sit." She directed me to the breakfast table which no longer contained a pile of her clothes. She returned to the kitchen counter and put the lid on a container.

"I'm going to bring this to the woman I told you about. You just make yourself at home. Feel free to check out the pub. Just enter through the double doors opposite the side entrance. I'll probably be back in an hour."

I mumbled something incomprehensible as my mouth was stuffed but she was already on her way.

The flan really was delicious. It didn't take me long to finish. I put the plate and spoon in the dishwasher and found the door to the pub.

It was a cosy space with brick walls, a wooden floor and plenty of booths and tables. There was a fireplace and a big bar. I walked around it to see plenty of space in the back as well. It led to double doors and there were more tables outside.

This place would be plenty popular during business hours, I imagined.

I ventured through a door at the side of the bar and entered the kitchen. To my amazement, it was spotless. Clearly, all her love and attention were poured into this area of the building.

My mother had been a bad cook. We mostly ordered take-out or had cereal or pancakes for dinner. She would pretend it was some great rebellious thing, to have a breakfast dinner, which worked when I was seven but got old pretty quickly.

What was that sound?

Water?

I returned to the front of the pub and spotted one of the beer taps gushing beer all over the bar. I dashed behind it and grabbed the tap, pushing it back. It jammed on something, and

I had to use sheer force before it finally shut off. There was beer everywhere. Ugh.

I turned to grab a tea towel and slipped on the floor, falling flat on my back with a thud.

Pain spread through my back and I winced, but at least my head was okay. I sighed and rested my head on the floor. I definitely needed another shower.

Betty's face came into view and she let out a "Baaa—" as if to laugh at me.

"Sadist," I said to her.

Chapter Two
The New Client

I ADJUSTED THE LIGHT blue dress and tugged on the white apron. Sure, I had gone a bit overboard since it wasn't the 1950s, but I figured someone who had statues of lions and a fountain with a large mermaid in the front garden would only like it.

I resembled a maid, and for all intents and purposes, I was one. I liked cleaning, so I didn't mind. The added bonus, of course, was that I had complete access to every nook and cranny of this Georgian estate. Not that I'd be stealing anything. If all went well, I'd be seeing a lot more of these places.

It was only a matter of time before I reached my intended target.

I pressed my index finger on the golden doorbell and took one steady breath. My auburn hair was tied up in a bun, and I touched it one more time. I don't know why I kept on doing that; it's not like it was going to fall off. In my other hand I had a cleaning caddy with my essential cleaning supplies.

The door opened and a woman with a gorgeous hour-glass figure opened the door. She had to be wearing a corset. I subconsciously sucked in my tummy and plastered a smile on my face.

The woman had medium-length platinum blonde hair and had speckled on lots of makeup. She wore a purple dress and was touching her golden necklace with a diamond.

The diamond was about two point sixty-five carat if I had to guess. The tiny diamonds surrounding the larger one were zero point fifteen carat at the most.

Her left ring finger sported a sapphire and diamond ring with a gold band. She lowered it as she looked me up and down, taking away my chance of a good look. Still, the diamond was probably one carat. Not bad at all, especially for an engagement ring. If only a rich bloke loved me like that.

"Clara McIntyre?" she asked in a sweet and low voice.

"Indeed I am." I didn't like shaking people's hands, but still I stuck out my hand. "Nice to meet you, Ms Pearbottom."

She wrinkled her nose at that. "Not for long, dear. And I don't shake hands because of germs."

"Oh, gotcha." At least that was one thing we had in common. Probably the only thing.

"I told you on the phone that I have one other maid. She should be here, but she's late." She stepped out of the way to let me in. When I did, she leaned in closer, forcing me to look into her cold, blue eyes.

"I don't like when people are late. I hope you won't see it as a reason to be late in the future." Her breath smelt like mojito even though it was only eleven o'clock in the morning.

"Don't worry, I'm punctual. My mother taught me that. She said that a punctual person is a professional person."

"Do I smell beer? And...livestock?" She raised an eyebrow.

I took a shower, but apparently it hadn't done much. "Err, yes. I'm staying at the pub and Betty, a sheep who lives in the garden there, had turned on a beer tap, I think. It was jammed, but I shut it off and then I fell. After that, Betty was mocking me so a battle ensued. I had to get her out of there and tried shoving, luring, yelling, begging, singing, and at some point I did a mime performance."

She narrowed her eyes at me as if to assess if I was joking. If only I was.

"Alright, then. As long as you don't drink on the job."

Ms Pearbottom moved to the table in the hallway. It contained a single vase. Crystal. My eyes widened as I realised it was Lalique crystal.

Those could be sold ranging from two thousand to ten thousand pounds. *Be still, my beating heart.*

"Anyway, I'm glad your mother taught you to be punctual. She sounds like a smart woman. Mine never taught me much. Just that I should get Botox when I turn thirty and that I should avoid carbs." She gave a wry smile. "Now, like I said over the phone, I just want you for the bathrooms and the kitchen. I've left the doors to the bathrooms open so you know where they are. The kitchen is at the back. If you want food or something to drink, make sure you bring your own stuff. Harriet, she's the other maid, she's hardly noticeable. I like it that way."

"I'll be a ghost, but less spooky."

The corner of her red lips quivered but didn't quite go up. "You're cute. If you need anything, let me know. I'll be around here somewhere, though I do have tennis practice in about an hour."

"Ah, tennis," I say. "That sounds nice. Do you play with friends?"

"No. Playing tennis is something you do with a hot instructor and then talk about with your friends afterwards."

She giggled when I gaped at her. "I'm joking, dear."

"Right, of course. Ha-ha." I couldn't wait to start cleaning.

"I had another maid, but she decided to move back home." Ms Pearbottom moved into another room, and I figured she wanted me to follow her.

The room contained a large bookshelf, two sofas, a fireplace and a table with drinks. She poured herself a mojito from a shaker. I was willing to bet she used to be a bartender, waiting to snatch herself a wealthy man. Smart.

I stood by the window and looked out over the front garden. It stretched until it reached iron gates in the distance. My blue Beetle was parked next to her Lexus. Probably a present from her fiancé.

She joined me. "Nice car, huh? It's not the car I wanted, though. He got me the one that *he* really liked." She shook her head and continued to complain about the fifty-five-thousand-pound car her man had gotten her.

But I was focussed on the ring on her finger.

In this light, it was clear that it was not a real diamond. Okay, not clear, but I had a good eye. It was too colourless to be real. Meaning her fiancé had bought her a fake ring. Why? I looked at the car she was still rambling about.

"What car did you have in mind?" I asked, interrupting her.

She raised her perfectly plucked eyebrows. "Don't make fun of me, but I actually wanted a vintage car. My dad was a huge fan, and I've always wanted one." Her eyes sparkled as she said these words, and she instantly looked a hundred times more attractive. She even smiled.

"Why would I make fun of you for that? Those are awesome cars. I would kill for a 1931 Duesenberg Model J Murphy." My mum was obsessed with anything vintage.

Her eyes widened. "Y—you like vintage cars too? Oh, my. Yes, that car is gorgeous. Personally, I really love the 1939 Alfa Romeo Lungo Spider. It's a classic sports car, and the engine is a 2.9 L straight-8."

I studied her face. "Your dad was a mechanic."

She blushed. "Yes. How did you know?"

"It's part of my job to read between the lines," I said.

She frowned. "As a maid?"

Oh, right. Oops. It had been so long, I needed to remember I was playing a role. "Yes, I guess. Anyway, bathroom, you said?"

She blinked rapidly, as if she only just now remembered why I was here. "Yes, sure." Her voice was softer now. I could tell she had warmed to me. That was good. I could use that.

"You're not who I thought you would be," she said with narrowed eyes.

"Right back at ya." I flashed her a smile. That was not a good thing. I needed her presumptions to match what she was seeing. I hurried upstairs. The staircase was broad and had a gorgeous red carpet that absorbed my footfalls.

"My name's Pearl, by the way," she called after me.

I looked over my shoulder. "It's nice to meet you, Pearl."

The corridor was broad and filled with endless doors. At least, that's how it seemed. I went left first and entered the first opened door. It was a large bathroom with a jacuzzi and a walk-in shower. It had two sinks with one large mirror and claw-foot bathtub. I was about to turn around and ask about the hoover when I saw it in the corner by the door. A cordless Dyson. I nearly groaned with pleasure.

I hoovered the floor first. Then I moved on to the bathtub and shower. I used white vinegar and baking soda for the shower tiles, which left them sparkly and white. I was sweating by the time I was mopping the floor when I felt someone watching me.

I turned around, expecting the other maid, but it was a handsome man with broad shoulders and a dimple in his chin. He wore a dark blue cardigan and white trousers. He grinned at me.

I didn't like the look in his eyes. He looked at me as if I was a chicken and he a hungry wolf.

"Hello," I said flatly, hoping my dismay was clear.

"Hi. I don't think I've seen you before."

"Are you Pearl's fiancé?" I asked.

His lips pulled into a straight line. "Yes, I am. Nathan Weatherby." He stepped into the bathroom with an outstretched hand.

"Dirty," I said as I held up my palm.

He stopped and lowered his hand. "Maybe I like it dirty."

Gross.

Someone cleared their throat behind him. He turned around, revealing a woman with dark hair and dark eyes. She glared at Nathan, while he looked back at me and shrugged.

"I guess I should leave you to it," he said, but avoided my gaze.

Nice to know he was capable of feeling guilt. He darted out of the bathroom. The other woman stared at him before turning her attention to me.

"I'm Harriet. You must be Clara," she said with a hint of hostility.

"I am. And thanks for rescuing me from that douchebag." I didn't want her to think I was interested in him or that I had made a move on him. If Pearl found out, she would fire me.

She clenched her jaw and looked away, but I saw the emotion in her eyes.

Interesting. Let's test my theory.

"Can you imagine being involved with such a sleaze? I mean, his fiancée is right downstairs."

She swallowed and jutted out her chin. "It's not our business. Let's just get to work." A blush spread out across her cheeks.

Yep. She was shagging the not-so-rich dude with the fiancée.

"Sure," I said.

She started working on the other bathrooms, which meant I didn't see much of her. I was looking forward to getting more information on Pearl and Nathan, though I wasn't sure if she would have given it to me. We had only just met and during that time I'd insulted her lover who had flirted with me.

I had forgotten how much fun rich people could be. The big cons always contained drama, and the ones you couldn't plan for were always the best.

The only thing I had to do here was make sure that Pearl would recommend me to others in her circle. If I did a good job and impressed her, I'd get where I wanted to be.

THREE HOURS LATER, I ventured down the stairs with a sore back and a sweaty forehead. Those bathrooms were as sparkly as a real diamond, and I felt proud. I'd just have to take a third shower when I got … home. It was weird to consider that place home, but it was. For now.

The best thing about this whole con was that I got to clean. It was so satisfying.

I wasn't sure if Harriet was done already, but I couldn't find her upstairs. I figured I'd get a start on the kitchen, if Harriet hadn't done that already.

I was also starving. It hadn't occurred to me to bring lunch. Normally, I was smarter than this, but the pranking sheep had distracted me. I hadn't even had a chance to explore the village.

The kitchen was at the back of the mansion, but as I was about to pass an open door to my left, I clearly heard Nathan's voice.

"I told you, I just need some more time."

"Time? You've proposed to her, which means you lied to me. And you were just hitting on the new maid," Harriet said.

Bingo.

"No, I wasn't. Did she say that? I'm not interested in her at all. Baby, you're all I care about, but we can't discuss this here and not now."

"Is that because your fiancée is walking around? There's an easy solution."

"Babe—" he started.

"It's time you choose. Her or me."

It felt like a final statement, so I took three steps back and started walking, just as she left the room. She didn't see me as she turned left, towards the kitchen.

I wasn't sure if Nathan would follow her, so I waited two seconds before heading in the same direction. I looked down at the floor as I carried my cleaning supplies and didn't glance into the room.

This was his place, and if he broke it off with Pearl, she wouldn't be needing my services. I certainly wouldn't want to work for this bastard, nor with his mistress if they kept things up. Still, knowing what I knew about rich people was that he wouldn't choose the maid. They never choose the help.

Harriet started scrubbing the floor while I worked on the counters. I even cleaned out the fridge and gave it a wipe. I used baking soda and vinegar on the oven and after it was clean, I put in a bowl of vanilla extract to make the whole place smell lovely.

Just as we finished, Harriet checked her phone and turned to me. "My boyfriend is here to pick me up. Do you mind if I hurry off?"

I managed to keep my expression blank. "Sure, no problem."

When she left, I needed a moment to wrap my head around this mess. She had a boyfriend but wanted to be with the rich douche, while the rich douche was just shagging her and intended to marry Pearl.

But why?

Pearl's dad was a mechanic so she didn't come from a rich family, and it seemed to me that Nathan was having money problems. Why else buy a fake diamond ring?

What was his endgame?

Then again, I shouldn't care. This was their mess, not mine. I was not getting involved.

Chapter Three
Getting Involved

I WAS STARVING AND ready to get myself a nice lunch. The pub would already be open, so that's where I was headed. First I'd change and put away my caddy with cleaning supplies. I parked across from the pub and got out.

A warm, male voice drew my attention. "Excuse me, Clara."

I turned to find the vicar walking my way. There was a slight limp as he walked, though it was barely noticeable. He smiled when he reached me and dimples appeared in his cheeks. He had chestnut hair that was receding and a friendly demeanour. I instantly liked him.

"Hello," I said.

"Hi, there. You must be Clara. I saw the cleaning supplies and the outfit and put two and two together. Agnes told me about you. Welcome to Greystone."

"Thanks, I appreciate it. It's a lovely village. I particularly like the omnivorous sheep with a penchant for mischief."

He chuckled. "Ah, yes. Betty. Agnes has a soft spot for her. Speaking of Agnes, you're in good hands. She's a terrible busybody, but she means well and always does her best to cheer people up and help them. You'll get along swimmingly, I'm sure."

"I'm sure we will."

"And as for any other information you might need, I'm Ignacius, the vicar. As you may have guessed. I have an artificial leg and am also part of the neighbourhood watch."

"Neighbourhood watch? Wait, also?" I frowned.

"I like how that part drew your attention," he said with a chuckle. "But yes, Agnes runs the neighbourhood watch. We always meet up in the pub and discuss...observations."

"So, gossip?" I asked with a smile.

"You're a smart one, aren't you? Yes, that's pretty much it. How long are you staying?"

"A few months. Just to see if my services as a maid are welcome here."

"Oh, I'm certain they are. You know, you should come to the service on Sunday, and I'll introduce you to everyone. It's the best way to get the word out about your work."

I imagined the rich snobs wouldn't set foot in the church, so there wasn't much of a point, but I couldn't exactly tell him that.

"Religion isn't really my thing," I said.

"Oh, I totally understand. It isn't mine either."

"What?"

"Do make sure you come. It will be such fun." He gave me a cheery wave and went back in the direction of the church.

Hmm. Interesting village so far.

On my way back, I'd weaved through the cobbled streets and past cute cottages and semi-detached homes with nice gardens. Some of the people who had been gardening waved at me even though they didn't even know me. I felt a stab of envy towards anyone who got to live in this village. Let alone grew up here.

This village was very different from bouncing around between hotels and bed and breakfasts. Worse were the homes from gullible people my mother was conning. I had never felt more ill at ease than at those places. The people were always friendly, and the guilt was ever present.

Some kids had imaginary friends. I had a shadow monster named Guilt to remind me I wasn't a good person.

THE PUB WAS QUIET. I had changed into my regular outfit and had taken a third shower, which hopefully wouldn't be the norm. I just had to avoid Betty.

Agnes was behind the bar, her cheeks flushed.

"Are you okay?" I asked, as I took place on one of the barstools.

"No, not at all. My bartender just quit because she found love or something silly like that, and now I have to work the bar and all the customers."

"Will it get busier?" I glanced around. There were only a handful of people.

"In a minute or so, yeah. Tonight, hell yeah." She shook her head. "I'm so screwed."

"I was a waitress once, as well as a bartender. I can help out if you're in a pinch, but I'd appreciate some food first. I forgot to bring lunch to my client, and if I don't eat soon, I'll keel over."

She stopped wiping the bar as her eyes twinkled. "You are the best," she said excitedly and rushed over to clasp my hands in hers.

I could only hope she washed her hands regularly. The gesture was kind, though. I liked seeing her light up like that. My mother would rarely look that happy. In fact, I couldn't even remember her looking that blissful. I mostly remembered fake smiles and charming fake laughs.

"What would you like? No, wait. I think I've got the perfect sandwich for you. Let me tell one of the chefs. Fun fact, all the people working in my kitchen are called Bob and all of them are bald." She threw her head back and laughed, and I wasn't sure if it was a joke or not.

More people trickled in, but it still wasn't too busy. Regardless, I ate my goat's cheese sandwich quickly. I wasn't sure how she knew I would like it, but I did. It was a pity I had to rush; I wanted to spend more time adoring it.

When I was done, I hurried behind the bar, put on a dark red apron and grabbed pen and paper. Together with Agnes, we made sure we got the new customers hydrated and fed.

It wasn't until two in the afternoon that things became quiet again. My legs were in pain and my back was sore. It didn't help that I'd had an intense morning; I wasn't used to cleaning five bathrooms in one morning.

I groaned as I slid into one of the booths.

Agnes chuckled. "Here's a water pitcher and a glass." She put it down in front of me, and I immediately poured myself a glass and downed it.

"How do you do this?" I asked her as I leaned back in the seat.

"With a lot of determination." She nudged my arm. "You did wonderful. You should be proud of yourself. If you want another job, consider yourself hired."

I looked up at her smiling face. It felt nice to be complimented. I realised then that my mother never even did. *Or do I just not remember?*

A frown formed between my eyebrows.

I could feel Agnes staring at me, so I looked up and thanked her.

She narrowed her eyes at me briefly, then curled her lips into a carefree smile. "Sure." Her head moved in the direction of the entrance, and she gave a cheery wave.

"Pavani, come meet your new neighbour," she said.

I was pouring another glass of water, so I couldn't turn around and scope her out as she was walking towards me. But I had to remind myself that it didn't matter. I had time to figure these people out. They were not my targets, even if I couldn't let my guard down.

The woman had a long black braid and was slender. She had some wrinkles, but I wouldn't have pegged her as being in her eighties. She gave me a firm handshake and introduced herself.

"Clara," I said, and returned the firm handshake.

"So, you're my new neighbour?" she asked in a cockney accent. She had on no jewellery whatsoever and wore bright yellow leggings and a purple shirt.

"I am. Just for a few months."

Agnes was still by our table, but left when someone approached the bar to order a drink.

"Where are you from?"

I repeated the same thing I'd told Agnes. Before she could grill me any further, I decided to turn the tables on her. The less these people knew about me, the better.

"How long have you been teaching yoga?" I asked.

"As long as I can remember. Are you interested?"

"I am. I've been practising it myself, but I'm self-taught. The internet is very handy."

Her round face instantly brightened as she smiled, as did her dark eyes. "Yes, but it doesn't beat the real thing. You should come some time. The first lesson is free."

"I'll think about it." But I had no intention of doing so. I wanted to keep my distance.

"No pressure. Your client is Nathan Weatherby, isn't it?"

My ears immediately perked up. "Yes, that's right. Well, his fiancée hired me. What do you know about them?"

Agnes approached our table to give Pavani a cup of mint tea. She hadn't even ordered anything, so that had to be her regular drink.

Agnes answered before Pavani could. "He's not fit to marry anyone, that one. He's reckless, always has been."

"In what way?" I kept my voice nonchalant, but really, I was so eager I could burst into confetti. It felt like we were school girls, gossiping. I had never had that experience, and this was surprisingly fun. And necessary. Information really was power, and I didn't trust Nathan Weatherby.

"He had driven his dad's car without a driver's license and crashed it. His dad ended up taking the blame. There's a rumour he knocked up his first girlfriend, but she moved away, so we can't be sure. He's also never had a real job, and I'm pretty sure he's spending money left and right. The only good thing he did was go to nursing school, but he quit that too. He probably joined so he could chase skirts." Agnes went on.

Naughty Nathan.

"What about Pearl? She seems nice," I said in my most innocent tone. Although, she really did seem nice.

"She seems like a bimbo, but that's just what Nathan would go for," Agnes said, eliciting a head shake from Pavani.

"What?" Agnes said to her.

"She's nice. I once met her in the shop, and we had a brief conversation about nothing special. I think she's lonely."

Me too. Which was only beneficial to me, but too bad for her.

"Are you joining the neighbourhood watch meeting?" Pavani suddenly asked as she fixed her eyes on me.

"I would, but I'm already beat. Is it okay if I join tomorrow? I am interested in joining." Since information was power, sticking close to the fiercest of gossipers in this village would be handy.

"Lovely," Pavani said. "It's nice to have fresh blood. And you, my dear, have a lovely aura."

I shrugged. "Well, they're all the rage these days."

Agnes let out a bark of laughter. "I told you she was fun."

I WAS SO BEAT THAT, despite my intention of taking a walk around the village, I ended up reading on the sofa until I had an early dinner and then went to bed.

The blinds were still closed in the opposite flat, and I was curious who was living there. I had stood leaning on the French balcony for ten minutes before finally turning in, and all I could stare at was my neighbour's place, divided by an alley. Unfortunately, I had only seen a vague outline once. It seemed to belong to a man, but that was all I could tell.

I wasn't sure what I was expecting, but after meeting an omnivorous sheep, an atheist vicar, and an eighty-year-old yogi, I had high hopes.

The next morning I found a lunch box outside my door with a post-it from Agnes.

I made you something yummy. Don't forget to eat. Xx A.

My eyes unexpectedly filled with tears, and I quickly wiped them away. Why was I crying over something like this?

I put the breadbox in my tote bag with elephants on it. I had once bought it because part of the proceeds went to a charity for elephants. In my other hand I carried my caddy with cleaning supplies and continued on my way to work.

When I parked my rattling Suzuki Alto next to Pearl's, I noticed a green Land Rover that wasn't here yesterday. Perhaps it belonged to Harriet or the gardener.

I rang the doorbell and Pearl opened the door again. The muscles in her neck and shoulders were tensed, and her mouth was set in a straight line as she was pressing her lips together. She did not look happy.

My heart skipped a beat. Had Harriet stirred up trouble for me?

"Thank you for being on time, Clara." She closed the door behind me.

"Is everything alright?" I asked, as an unfamiliar male voice drifted our way from the adjacent room, the one where Pearl and I chatted yesterday.

"No, everything is not alright. Harriet didn't come home last night, according to her boyfriend, and this police detective is asking all her clients what they know. As if we have anything to do with her dereliction of duty."

A detective asking questions was definitely not ideal. But why send a detective when they didn't suspect foul play? Usually people had to wait twenty-four hours before even being allowed to report someone missing.

"Is this unusual for her?" I asked.

"How would I know? Maybe she just left her boyfriend."

"But she's never disappeared before?"

She gave me a smile that didn't reach her eyes. "You sound like the detective. I'm sorry you have to do everything on your own today. You did a good job yesterday, so I appreciate your help. If you could do the rest of the bathrooms today and half of the bedrooms, that would be wonderful."

I beamed with pride. "Thanks for the compliment. I like working for you." It wouldn't hurt to suck up, though on the inside I was dreading to do two bathrooms and six bedrooms in one morning.

She gave me a genuine smile this time. "Silly girl," she said with affection, even though we were the same age.

I went up the stairs as she disappeared into the next room while my polite smile vanished. What had Harriet gotten herself into? Did this have anything to do with Nathan? Or was she just fed up with it all? Perhaps Nathan had broken things off and she'd decided to leave.

I shook my head. It didn't matter. Although, it still bothered me that a detective had come out. Had they found signs of foul play? Was he going to dig for information about me?

Harriet really had stirred up trouble for me.

I went straight to the end of the hall and would work my way towards the middle. I'd do the bedrooms last. At least I had a nice home-made lunch to look forward to.

As soon as I entered the bathroom, my eyes were drawn to the walls, and I stood frozen. My legs started shaking at the sight.

Blood was smeared on the walls.

Chapter Four
First Suspicions

I BACKED OUT OF THE bathroom. Pearl's melodious laughter rang through the corridor, and it meant they were all coming up. I had expected that. If I were that detective, I'd want to speak to me.

I leaned against the wall and slid down while I screamed as loudly as I could. I was upset, sure, but I needed to be extra upset. The more they saw me as a meek woman, the better. From the corner of my eye, I saw them running.

I didn't look at them, didn't move. I simply pointed to the bathroom. A man with a long, grey trench coat stopped in the door opening and then took a few steps inside while Pearl crouched down next to me and stroked my arm.

She glanced into the bathroom right as Nathan blocked her view.

"What's going on?" she asked with a shaky voice.

"There's blood on the walls," the detective said in a rough voice. "I need you all to stay away while I call this in." He bent down in front of me and looked me in the eyes.

He had sandy hair, a rugged but charming air about him, and a scar on his upper lip. "Why don't you take your time in one of these bedrooms; drink some water, calm down, and I'll come see you in a minute, okay?"

I nodded and purposely made my bottom lip tremble.

Pearl helped me to my feet, and we disappeared into the closest bedroom. I managed to steal a glance at Nathan, who showed no emotions whatsoever. His face was blank.

Interesting.

"Was there really blood on the walls?" Pearl asked as she directed me towards the large double bed. The room was decorated in red and golden accents. My mother would have loved it.

"Yeah. Like someone had been attacked in there." I glanced at Pearl, who looked a shade paler.

She nodded pensively. "I'm sorry you had to see that. I don't understand at all. Why would there be blood in a bathroom that is rarely used? And how could that have happened? Nobody else is here besides Nathan and I."

"But me and Harriet were here yesterday," I said. "Maybe you have other people who have access to this place?"

"The gardener and chef, but they weren't here yesterday. Also, you don't have a key yet. Harriet does."

Good. That left me in the clear. Harriet left with her boyfriend yesterday, but if she had a key so she could have easily come back. Maybe she and Nathan fought and he cut her? But why in that guest's bathroom? And why would anyone have a knife on them? Unless this was Harriet's way of taking revenge. She could have done this to herself to make Nathan look bad. Or even Pearl. But why?

It would be easy to figure that out by checking her for wounds when she showed up. I glanced at Pearl's forearms. No cuts.

"Pearl," I said.

"Yeah?" She had been staring into the distance, but now focussed on me. "Sorry, I'll get you some water."

"No, no. I just wanted to ask you...why is that detective here?"

"Ian Clarke," she said. "And he's here because Harriet's boyfriend reported her missing. I told you that."

"No, but why is he here? He's a homicide detective. They don't come out to question people unless they suspect foul play."

She raised her thin eyebrow at me.

"I heard that on TV," I quickly added.

She frowned, her eyes darkening. "I—I don't know. I didn't think about that." She sat down next to me. "This is bad. I already have a shaky reputation. I don't need this."

"Nobody needs this," I said, a little too sharp.

She looked up at me and chuckled dryly. "You must think I'm quite shameless. I know that's what most people think. The thing is, it's not easy being in Nathan's world with a dad who's a mechanic and when I, myself, was a bartender. Even my friends aren't really my friends. They just stay close to me so they can gossip about me. I have to always be on guard around them."

I knew a little something about that.

"That must be lonely," I said, knowing it was.

She nodded. "Yeah, well. I don't think Harriet's in danger. I don't think anyone is in danger. It's a very disturbing prank."

"That Harriet executed?" She had to have an idea of who Harriet was and what she was capable of. Would she have done something like this?

She shrugged. "I don't know her well enough to say for sure, but she had been weird around me lately."

"Weird, how?"

"She didn't look me in the eye anymore. I know that sounds silly, but it's true. And sometimes she'd chat with me, but she'd also stopped doing that."

I bit my tongue. It would probably come out, wouldn't it? If she stayed missing much longer. Or worse, if it turned out to be her blood.

"Pearl," I started, but then there was a knock and the detective stood in the door opening. He glanced at Pearl.

"Miss, would you mind waiting downstairs with your fiancé?" he asked.

"Not at all," she said and squeezed my arm. "Will you be okay?"

I nodded. "Thanks."

He waited until Pearl was gone and left the door open. Probably so he could make sure nobody entered the bathroom.

"I'm DS Ian Clarke," he said and stepped into the middle of the room.

"Clara McIntyre." It had become easy so quickly to say that name. I hopped off the bed and smoothed my dress. My mother had always taught me to bring attention to my body when talking to a man. She was the queen of making people underestimate her.

"I'm so terribly sorry I screamed," I said and touched my cheeks. "I'm so embarrassed." I looked down at the floor, then glanced up at him.

He gave a small smile. "Don't worry about it. It must have been quite the shock."

"It's not something you expect to find." I took a few steps forward while I scanned his outfit. Black shoes that had lost their shine, grey trousers that were nice, but not expensive, and a white shirt and grey jacket that were similarly nice but cheap. Two top buttons undone, no tie or jewellery, though he did have a tan line on his ring finger. Recently divorced or widowed.

When I got closer, I could smell a very nice aftershave. Calvin Klein?

I put my hand on my chest. "I hope nobody has been seriously hurt. What do you think happened?"

He studied my face. "I'm trying to find out. When did you last see Harriet Briggs?"

"Yesterday. At the end of our shift. We were in the kitchen, and I wanted to get to know her a bit better; it was my first day, after all. But then a car horn sounded, and she said it was her boyfriend coming to pick her up. She left, and I left soon thereafter. Didn't see her again."

"Did anything seem strange or unusual about her? I know you don't know her, but did you get a bad or weird feeling at any point?"

I ran a finger across my bottom lip very slowly as I looked down at his shirt, thinking. I could feel his gaze on my mouth.

If I told him about Nathan, it would definitely put me on his radar. Would I have to give a formal statement at the police office? Would my name be in records? And whether or not Nathan was involved, I'd definitely not be working here anymore. I needed this job, and I needed a good recommendation. Exposing a client as a cheater would not be good word-of-mouth.

Then again, if she had been killed, why leave blood on the walls? It could have easily been cleaned.

Something weird was going on. And I couldn't get involved.

"Nothing I can think of, DS Clarke."

He narrowed his eyes at me, as if assessing me. "Call me Ian."

"Ian," I said. Ha, see. It was working. "Well, maybe you can tell me something. Why did you come all the way out here when her boyfriend only just reported her missing? You investigate murders, don't you?"

His eyes were dark and deep, ready to suck anyone in. There was a warmth in his eyes that I didn't see often, but also a sadness.

The corners of his lips only briefly pulled upwards. "The boyfriend is the son of my landlord. I was doing him a favour."

Ah, right. That's how villages work.

"I hope she's okay. I didn't know her, but I really hope she's okay," I said softly as I looked down at my hands. I did actually mean those words, even if I was laying it on a bit thick.

"Hmm," Ian just said.

I looked up at him. He didn't seem impressed by my damsel-in-distress routine. Perhaps I had to be a bit more subtle. He was in work mode, after all.

"What happens now?" I asked.

"We're processing the bathroom as a crime scene, and there's a CSI team on the way to analyse the blood. Better safe than sorry. Harriet is not the type to just disappear, and this blood is just too...it's just not right."

Damn straight.

"So, does this mean I can't continue my work?" It was a dumb question, which is why I asked it.

"No, you can't work."

"Do I go home?"

He sighed and looked around the room as if the answer could be found there. "You'd only just met her, even if there's foul play involved, it's unlikely you have anything to do with it." He turned his gaze back on me. "But—" his voice trailed off. "Where are you staying?"

Oh, damn. Was he really suspicious? Why?

"The pub."

His eyebrows shot up. "You're staying with Agnes. Right. She had mentioned that a few days ago. In that case, you can go home." In a lower voice he said, "I know where to find you."

I don't know if it was supposed to sound threatening or not, but to me it just sounded sexy. With that voice, anything kind of sounded sexy.

Maybe I could get him to list baked goods. That would be divine.

"Okay," I said and placed my hand on his chest. "That makes me feel a lot safer." Before he could respond, I moved past him and went into the corridor to retrieve my caddy and tote bag.

"What's in the bag?" Ian asked as he started walking next to me.

"A big cleaver. Want to see?" I said, automatically.

His head shot in my direction, one corner of his mouth tugging upwards.

I bit my lip to keep from grinning. I could only slip once.

"I see the shock is wearing off."

"I'm sure you had a hand in that. You have a very nice presence." It wasn't a lie. I would have immediately noticed him in a room filled with people. It wasn't his face or body, or anything like that. It was the way he carried himself.

I could tell he was studying me, but I continued looking ahead. We had reached the stairs.

"I'll go and say bye to Pearl," I said as I turned to him.

He handed me his card. "I'll see you soon."

"I look forward to it." My tone was matter-of-fact. I wasn't sure what the look he gave me meant, whether it was positive or negative, but I went down the stairs and found Pearl by the window with another cocktail. Just like yesterday, except she didn't look as relaxed as she had then. It was like dark clouds had gathered above her head. Did she know Nathan had been cheating on her? Had she done something to Harriet? But again, why not clean it up?

I glanced at Nathan. He was lying on the sofa with his iPad. He didn't seem bothered at all. I could feel Ian behind me and walked over to Pearl.

I touched her back to draw her out of her head. "Hey. Thanks for taking care of me. I'm heading to my flat now. If you need anything, please let me know. I'm here for you."

She frowned at me. "There's nothing to be concerned about. I'm sure it will be fine." Then her eyes softened. "But thank you. Make sure you take good care of yourself."

"I will."

I turned to look at Nathan who gave me a wave without looking up, and I tried not to glare at him. Ian escorted me to the front door and just as he opened it, several cars pulled up, including a police car. This would definitely bring about gossip.

I glanced back at Pearl who downed her drink.

"Take care," Ian said in that gruff voice.

I nodded at him and left.

I HURRIED BACK TO MY flat, and noticed my hand was shaking when I put my key in the lock. I was sure Agnes was up, but I hadn't seen her. I had been quiet getting up the stairs because I wasn't sure if I wanted to share what had happened. Not yet, anyway. Tonight, I would see how useful the neighbourhood watch would be.

Chapter Five
The Neighbourhood Watch

I ATE LUNCH EARLY IN my flat. Agnes had made me another goat's cheese sandwich and had added a blueberry muffin as well. She really knew how to bring a smile to my face.

I knew it would get busy around noon again, and I wanted to help Agnes out. She had been nice to me, and if gossip spread as fast as I thought, I might learn something beneficial.

Ten minutes before noon, I went downstairs. Just as I was about to go through the door, I froze. I turned to my left and made eye-contact with Betty.

"Oh, it's you again. What are you plotting now?"

The sheep simply blinked at me.

Just as I was about to get her outside, she turned around. As she did, she knocked over a coat rack that fell right on top of me. I fought with a bunch of coats, but finally succumbed to the floor.

I shouted in anger and tried to kick off the coat rack. I managed to come up for air, but I had a yellow hat on my head and two coats in my lap.

"I hate you!" I shouted after Betty, who let out a mocking "baaa."

After I had put everything back in place, I stomped into the pub. Agnes was just bringing some food to Pavani and a woman with dark-blond hair.

About seven tables were occupied, so I had made it just in time for the oncoming rush hour.

"Clara McIntyre, reporting for duty," I said to Agnes.

As soon as she noticed me, she rushed over. "Dear, are you alright? I heard about what happened this morning."

I could tell she actually cared. Unless she was very skilled at faking concern, but I doubted that. "Yes, it was quite the shock. I do feel better now."

"Why didn't you tell me this morning? I would have made you some nice herbal tea to relax." Agnes eyebrows were drawn up so high, they had the danger of disappearing into her hair.

"I just wanted to be alone and process everything. It was very strange."

"I can imagine." She rubbed my arm affectionately. "Don't worry. You don't have to help me, you can just—"

"Oh, no. Please, I need to do something." I looked at her, pleading.

She pursed her lips, then nodded. "Okay. After the lunch rush we'll have some nice tomato soup together."

I couldn't help but smile. "I'd like that."

Lines around her eyes formed as she grinned at me. "Good. Let's kick some butt then. And don't worry about what happened today. We'll discuss it at the neighbourhood watch meeting. I'm sure the truth will come out soon." We made it over to the bar, where I put on the apron again and grabbed a pen and paper.

"Wait, does this mean you met Ian?" Her eyes shone brighter as she peered at me.

Was it my imagination or did she look too excited?

"Err, yeah. DS Clarke."

She waved a hand. "I'm sure you can call him Ian. What did you think of him?"

Yep, she was definitely excited.

I felt a strange emotion as I realised she was playing matchmaker. I wasn't sure how I felt about that. The only experience I had in romance was...well, complicated. I didn't have good taste in men. Or perhaps it was because of the world my mother had brought me into.

That was, until I broke away.

I'd had a lot of shitty jobs, trying to make an honest living. But I had to. I'd nearly died once because I'd gotten involved with the wrong people. Still, surviving on my own hadn't been easy. It still wasn't. My mother had been on the wrong side of the law, but even when I got away for that very reason, it wasn't easy to survive with barely anything but principles.

"He seems clever." I cleared my throat. "I mean, cute." That was probably a better answer. A more innocent one. Also, if she thought I liked him, she wouldn't be suspicious. Only shifty people avoided the police.

She snapped her fingers. "I knew it. I think you guys would really hit it off. He needs someone in his life, you know? He's too focussed on the job ever since he—"

Got a divorce.

"—got divorced."

I smirked to myself. "Well, he is very handsome and charming." Okay, perhaps I was going too far now, but all Agnes did was beam with every word.

"Wonderful. And you're quite the catch as well."

I felt myself blush.

"Can I set you guys up then?"

My heart raced at the suggestion. It would be risky, but it would also be a good opportunity to find out more about Harriet and to gain favour with him. Assuming the date would go well. "Sure," I said.

Had I even been on a real date? Officially? Ever?

My heart started racing for a different reason now.

"Only if he's game, of course," I added quickly. Not sure if I hoped he would say yes, or not.

"Oh, he will be." She wiggled her eyebrows at me.

I chuckled. Agnes wasn't who I thought she would be. So far, nobody was.

The lunch crowd showed up soon enough and again, I was walking back and forth taking orders as well as tending the bar for those who wanted a pint. Nobody really drank anything else, though there was one woman who ordered a glass of wine.

So far, people were suspiciously quiet when I reached their table, and I wondered how much they knew about me and what had happened that morning. In the end, only two women asked me if I was okay, as well as what had happened. I had played dumb and stuck to vague answers, much to their dismay.

Gossip was probably normal for the people here, but I didn't like giving out information.

Information was power.

Pavani was there for lunch again, and this time the vicar had joined her. I barely had time to say hi to him and was already on to the next customer.

My cheeks felt warm, and I was sure they were red. Still, I liked helping out. When it started quieting down, a few people even introduced themselves to me. It made me feel welcome.

At some point, I looked up in time to see Agnes talk to Ian, who had apparently entered. She was talking animatedly when he glanced in my direction and our eyes met.

My body instantly felt warmer. I wasn't sure why I was this nervous. It's not like I actually liked him, even if I did like the idea of going on a date.

My mother had always maintained that romance didn't exist. That's why I probably had so many romance novels on my e-reader. And why I'd put up with so much crap from my ex.

I probably was expecting too much of this date already. Reality was never the same as fantasy. This would bite me in the ass.

Hopefully, he'd say no.

Agnes darted over to a couple that was about to leave and chatted with them for a while as Ian strode over to the bar and leaned against it.

"What can I get you?" I managed to keep my voice level.

He grinned as if he was going to make a joke, but instead cleared his throat. "An iced tea, please."

I went and got it for him.

"How are you feeling?" he asked.

"Much better now, thanks." I gave a half-smile.

He nodded and took a sip of his drink and continued to stare at it. "I heard you want to go on a date with me."

"And you believed it, huh? More's the pity." I shook my head in mock disappointment.

The corner of his mouth curled up. "This is the first time Agnes is trying to set me up, but it doesn't surprise me. She's responsible for a few weddings."

"As long as it's not funerals."

"Agreed. So, you don't want to go on a date then?" This time, he looked right at me with a penetrative stare.

I shrugged. "I'm only here for a few months, but I wouldn't decline a meal with a handsome man."

"Handsome, huh?" He took another swig of his drink. "Well, until this thing with Harriet is solved, I don't think it's a good idea to date, but we could have lunch here tomorrow. If you want."

His gaze seemed more intense as it swept over my face.

"I will have to visit a bunch of potential clients."

"An early lunch," he said.

Hmm. He was clearly eager to spend time with me. I still had it. Mother would be proud.

"Okay. I look forward to it. And I hope you'll figure out what's going on with Harriet soon. Will I be able to go to work tomorrow?"

"Yes. Just be careful."

"Why would you say that?" I hadn't thought I was at risk working there, but now that he said it like that...

"Until we know for sure what happened, just be careful." He finished his drink and put too much money on the bar. "Keep the change."

Agnes intercepted him on the way out, he said a few words, she beamed, and then he kissed her on the cheek and left.

She practically skipped over. "I'm going to make sure you guys have a lovely lunch."

How could she be this happy about it? She hardly even knew me. Didn't it occur to her that he could do way better than me?

"I appreciate that."

The rest of the afternoon, I did a deep clean of my kitchen and even defrosted the freezer. Afterwards, I took a shower. If only I could have scrubbed my mind clean of the macabre image of that blood smeared on the walls.

Agnes had invited me to have dinner in the pub, so around six I went downstairs again. Pavani was helping her out this time. She gracefully weaved her way through the area and brought plates and drinks over. It was captivating to watch. There was an elegance about her that made me envious.

I was grateful to sit down and chose a spot by the window, overlooking the cobbled square with the fountain in the middle. It was a small one with two stone benches on opposite sides.

Without having ordered, Agnes herself brought out a plate of fish and chips with gravy and small pieces of onion. "This is my signature dish. Enjoy."

"Thanks."

"I've also made you a dessert, so make sure to save room."

"Wow. You really spoil me."

She blushed. "I like cooking for people. I want my food to bring a smile to their faces and make them forget their worries. If only just temporarily."

She really was a sweet woman. "I get that."

"I had a feeling you might." She patted me on the arm and returned to the bar. There were a lot more men drinking pints now.

I glanced around. All these people seemed to be enjoying a nice, quiet life with friends and family. Instead of envy, I just felt a pain in my chest.

The fish and chips looked absolutely mouth-watering. Maybe it would make me feel better. I had never really sought comfort in food, I mostly escaped into books, but perhaps that was because my mother had never been a cook, nor had she taught me how to cook.

I took a bite and closed my eyes, wishing I could absorb the flavours. It took me a couple more bites before I realised I was smiling. Agnes could work magic.

Normally, I ate with the TV on in the background but now it didn't even occur to me to grab my phone. I didn't rush and savoured every bite.

I finished the whole meal.

When Agnes took my plate, she was grinning at me. "I could tell you liked it."

"I didn't like it. I loved it. There was not one thing I didn't like. It was gorgeous."

She giggled. "You flatter an old woman. I'll bring your dessert out in a short while."

"Okay."

Dessert was a crème brulee. I don't know how she knew that was my favourite, but it was. Although I had never had one that was as good as hers.

After it quieted down in the pub and the sun was setting, Pavani and the dark blond woman she was with earlier came in and sat down at my table.

Agnes had already set down a pot of tea and a couple of cups. It was neighbourhood watch time.

Pavani introduced me to Marilyn, a woman in her twenties. She had her thin hair in a ponytail and wore all black.

"Nice to meet you," Marilyn said in a soft voice. "You had quite the morning."

"You can say that again. I guess the whole village knows by now." I poured them both a cup of mint tea.

"Oh, yes. It is a hot topic," Pavani said.

"But no news?" I hadn't wanted to ask Ian, and maybe they knew more by now.

"Nothing new on Harriet, no. She hasn't used her phone since last night, nor her bank card. It's highly suspicious."

"She's a police officer," Pavani said to me, in order to explain how she knew that.

"I see." That meant it was likely she was dead. "But if she was killed, why the blood on the walls? And if she was murdered there, there would have been more traces."

Pavani nudged Marilyn. "Told you she was smart. It's in the eyes," she said.

Marilyn nodded. "Good. Then you will be a welcome addition to the team."

"Speaking of which, where is the rest of the team?"

At that moment, the vicar approached us.

"Hello, lovely ladies," he said and sat down. "How are you, dear?" he said to me.

"I'm okay now. Just had a strange morning. I hope Harriet's okay." I felt like I was becoming a record.

"Me too. God—or whoever—works in mysterious ways. If you believe in fate at all, that is," Ignacius said.

Agnes brought a plate of biscuits and clapped Ignacius on his back. "Good to see you, Iggy."

"I just saw you yesterday," he said. "Aren't you getting sick of my face?"

She grinned at him. "Never."

Clearly they were all good friends. I wondered if spending time with them would only make me feel more alone.

"Why don't you get our final member?" Agnes asked, and I realised a second too late that she was talking to me.

"Oh, what?"

"Our final member is at the cemetery by the church." She wiggled her eyebrows at me.

"I'm sorry. You want me to get a corpse?"

They all laughed.

"What?"

"He is practically a corpse, yeah, but don't worry, it will all become clear when you meet him. Go to the cemetery. He wants to introduce himself there."

I raised an eyebrow. "This sounds weird. Why is everyone so weird?"

"Baaah," Betty bleated and we all turned to discover her standing by the bar. She nudged one of the men off his stool, who then fell backwards into someone else, who fell against a chair, sliding it in the path of a group of women who were on their way out. One woman fell right over it, and like dominoes, the rest of the ladies tumbled over each other, creating a pile of flailing women.

"I rest my case," I said.

Chapter Six
Nosferatu

THE SUN WAS SETTING and the sky was dark with a mixture of purple and pink swirls. It wasn't too chilly out, even though there was a gentle breeze. I had no idea what kind of person would want to introduce themselves at a cemetery, but I was prepared to punch him.

I walked past a few people who greeted me as if they knew me. I greeted them back. Since gossip clearly spread fast, I had to be careful around the neighbourhood watch gang.

They seemed to mean well, but if they gossiped about others, they would gossip about me. I couldn't let my guard down.

The gate to the cemetery squeaked as I pushed it open. It was getting darker by the minute.

"Hello?" I said loudly. *Any weirdos here?*

I kept on walking until I reached the oak tree in the middle of the cemetery. I didn't imagine anyone would pop out from behind the gravestones, so— A twig snapped.

It came from behind the tree. I crossed my arms and turned around.

A man had his face mostly covered by a dark piece of cloth. I squinted and realised he was wearing a cape.

"Hello, Clara."

Not what I was expecting, but okay.

"Why are you creeping up on me? Men have died for less."

He chuckled, but it turned into a cough, and he was forced to lower his arm. He was easily in his nineties, with white hair and a wrinkled face. He coughed out his vampire teeth and shoved them back into his mouth before he properly faced me.

"My name," he said dramatically, "ish Noshferatu!" He spoke with a lisp and held his hands above him like claws, as if he was ready to pounce.

If he tried anything, I'd kick him in his bulbs of garlic.

"Hi, Joe," a man shouted at him and waved. His poodle looked up and tilted its head as it observed the old man dressed as a vampire. The man tugged on its leash, forcing it to move on before it could decide if it was scared or not.

Joe's shoulders slumped. "Okay, my name ish Joe."

"I had no idea," I said dryly. "And why are you lurking about in a cemetery, dressed as a vampire?"

He put a hand to his chest as he frowned in surprise. "Why, becaushe I am one."

"You're a vampire?"

"Yesh, of courshe."

I wasn't sure if he was delusional or pulling my leg. Maybe both.

"Vampires don't exist," I said.

He took out his vampire teeth. "How do you know? Is the Wunderpus photogenicus an animal?" His lisp was now gone. "Does the Spiny Lumpsucker exist? What about the Hellbender or Tasseled Wobbegong?"

I bit my lip to keep from laughing. "Right. Good point."

"Just because you've never seen them, or even heard of them, doesn't mean they don't exist. Besides, look at me. I'm ninety-three and I look amazing." He put his hands on his sides, striking a pose.

He looked like he was ninety-three.

I also spotted a wedding ring. "And what does your wife think of you lurking around in a cemetery?"

He lowered his hands and glanced in the direction of one of the tombstones.

Oh.

I got a jolt of sadness. No wonder he was worried about his mortality, although I had never encountered anyone who took it quite the way he did. An obsession with vitamins and exercise, sure, but hanging out at a cemetery dressed as a vampire, no.

"My wife chose to remain a mortal. It is quite the romantic, yet tragic love story." He gave a wry smile.

"I believe that," I said, and flashed him a sincere smile. "Why don't you tell it to me sometime?"

His eyes sparkled. "Really?"

"Of course. Are you ready for our neighbourhood watch meeting?"

He put his vampire teeth back in. "I shertainly am. Let me eshcort you." He held out his arm.

"A gentleman vampire. I have always wanted to meet one." I took his arm as we left the cemetery and went on our way to the pub.

We got no funny looks on the way, so as I thought, people knew about him well enough. How could they not? In a small village like this, such behaviour stood out.

I also figured he joined the neighbourhood watch in order to still have some connection to other people. He had to be lonely otherwise. Still, I wanted to ask, curious what he would say.

"Why'd you join the neighbourhood watch?"

He glanced over at me and took out his fake teeth again. "It is my duty as the only vampire in this village to take care of everyone here and make sure they are safe. It's important to stay informed. Knowledge is power."

"You've got that right," I mumbled.

"What about you? Why are you interested? I heard you were only staying for a few months."

"Yes, I'm just trying to find my place in this world. Figured I would see if I could make my living here. I've only recently started cleaning for a living."

"And how did you land here? There are plenty of other cute villages."

Despite his old age and eccentric dress-up preferences, there was a sharpness in his blue eyes. It just went to show I couldn't let my guard down in front of anyone. Not even someone like him.

"It took me a while to find a place I could afford, yet had rich clients in its vicinity." The hint of a grin balanced on my lips.

He chuckled. "Ah, yes. Rich clients are better than poor clients. And if you're looking for a home, you've found it here. This is a warm place. Especially when you've been out in the cold."

My head jerked up at him. Something about the way he stared off into the distance made me think he wasn't talking about me. Good. Otherwise my poker face had gotten way worse than I thought.

We reached the pub. There were still a few regulars, but Agnes seemed ready to focus on our meeting. She had put a variety of cheeses in front of the table and made sure everyone had drinks.

She seemed to really enjoy making people happy with food.

"There you are," she said with a broad smile on her face. "I see you've met Nosferatu."

At this, the others chuckled. It wasn't in a way that made me think they were mocking him. It was more as if they were teasing him. The way friends do.

"Yes, I've met the prince of darkness. Joe." I patted Joe on the back.

This elicited another chuckle from the others, including Joe.

I sat back down in my seat, taking a sip of my tea, which was now cold. The booth was big enough to hold all six of us. Ignacius was between me and Joe, while Agnes sat next to Pavani and Marilyn.

"Welcome to your first meeting, Clara," Agnes said. She raised her glass. "Here's to many more."

We all raised our tea cups and clinked them together.

"Thanks. I appreciate that."

"I think our first topic of the day will be Harriet," Agnes said.

Everyone pulled out a notebook.

"What are we doing?" I asked.

"We like to take notes and collect all information when something like this happens," Pavani said.

"So this happens often?" I ask.

"No," Ignacius answered. "We've only had minor crimes, like theft, or vandalism. We take notes then too. We just like to be thorough. We stopped a group of thieves last year and made the local papers."

"You did?" That was impressive.

"We also found out who stole Mr Furlough's duck," Joe said, to which Marilyn shivered.

"What's wrong?" I asked her. "Was it an evil duck?"

Her eyes widened. "Don't say that." She glanced around as she bit her lip.

The vicar leaned closer to me. "Don't mind her. She's got a bunch of phobias and Anatidaephobia is one of them."

"What kind of phobia is that?"

"The fear that somehow, somewhere, a duck is always watching you."

Marilyn clutched her hands over her ears. "That's enough. Stop talking about them." She shook her head and then lowered her hands slowly.

"Speaking of which, don't wear yellow around her. She's got a phobia about that too," Ignacius added.

"I see." I didn't see. Not even a little bit. I had no idea phobias like this existed.

"That's why I usually don't go out when it rains. Too many people wear raincoats that are...of a certain colour," Marilyn said, blushing.

"And what did you do again?" I asked.

"I'm a police officer."

"Right."

We moved on to the case of the missing maid. Parvani was able to give us a lot of details about Harriet since her mother was in her yoga class. She had finished secondary school, but had never been serious about education. Instead, she'd had various jobs until she settled on becoming a maid. She liked the work and had only recently started working for the more privileged clients. She was also quite spoiled, and it was a source of tension between her and her boyfriend.

"Do you think she had bad intentions, working for the richer people?" Ignacius asked.

Pavani tilted her head. "Her mother was worried she'd see what it was like on the other side, and that she might become desperate to achieve such a lifestyle."

"Desperate enough to romance a certain rich bloke?" I asked.

They all looked at me.

"Why do you say that?" Agnes asked.

I couldn't tell them what I knew because it would certainly get back to the detective. "It seems the most logical thing to do. If she were to steal from her clients, they'd find out soon enough. The only thing she can do is marry someone who is rich. Pearl's doing the same thing. Though it is possible she actually likes Nathan." I couldn't see why, but there was a chance she did.

"Good point," Marilyn said. "We should make a list of all her clients and see if anyone might have been eligible enough to grab her attention."

Between all five of them, they managed to make a list of seven clients. That was actually impressive. Not all of them were wealthy clients, but a lot of them were.

My heart started beating faster as I studied the list. I took out my phone and copied the names.

"Even if she wasn't cheating on her boyfriend or up to something bad, those clients might know something useful. Perhaps something they wouldn't tell the police," Ignacius said.

Agnes leaned forward. "You know, these people are all desperate for a maid. It's a good thing we have one right here."

I smirked. "You know what? I was thinking exactly the same thing."

We then went through everything else we knew, which wasn't much. Except that Marilyn had an interesting bit of news she'd been sitting on.

"It will come out tomorrow, so I might as well tell you," she said. "The blood on the walls is human, and they're currently checking to see if it's hers."

There was a collective gasp even though we all kind of figured it would be.

How did it get there? Where was her body? I couldn't help but think it didn't add up.

"Maybe it was a vampire," Joe said. "Or aliens."

"In this village, it wouldn't surprise me," I said, intending to keep that in my head.

Pavani chuckled. "I get that. Especially with Betty so close."

"Don't worry. She'll grow on you," Agnes said with a wink.

The rest of the meeting quickly turned to regular village-life gossip. I learned that a Mrs Oblonsky collected toothpicks and used them to build miniature houses. A Mr Morris was still at it—meaning he was still gardening naked, and a woman named Frannie was so desperate for a husband that she had crocheted one.

I helped Agnes close up during closing time, and even spotted a few of the Bobs working in the kitchen. They were all bald but couldn't have been more different in size; both height and width.

"Did you enjoy yourself?" Agnes asked as we went through the double doors into the private area. She had switched off the lights in the pub and locked the main entrance.

"This is an interesting village," I said.

"It is certainly entertaining. And I'm glad it made you smile. You're very beautiful when you smile."

I gaped at her. "T—thank you." Why would she say that?

"I mean sincerely," she added. "I sometimes think you aren't able to do that a lot." She had a line between her eyebrows as she said this.

"Why do you think that?" I kept my voice level.

She shrugged. "I guess I went through a difficult time as well, a time when I smiled to reassure everyone I was okay but really wasn't. I couldn't have children, you see. Nothing to be done about it, but I was very depressed. I'm okay now, but I recognise polite smiles from a mile away. Not that there's anything wrong with them. You can't help the way you feel and how you want to portray yourself to the outside world. I just—I just hope you can find happiness here."

I curled my hands into fists. "Why would you even assume I deserve happiness? What if I'm a terrible person?"

She placed her warm hand on my cheek. "Darling, I can also spot a terrible person from a mile away. You're definitely not one. There's a difference between doing something terrible and being terrible, in case you're confusing the two. Don't forget that." She pinched my cheek and sauntered off towards the kitchen.

Perhaps she was right.

No. The reason I was here proved she wasn't.

And I wasn't going to abandon my mission. I couldn't.

Chapter Seven
A Lunch Date

THE NEXT MORNING, NATHAN opened the door instead of Pearl. He had one hand stuffed in his pocket and a self-satisfied smirk on his face. I couldn't imagine why.

After my lunch with the detective, I was going to visit the other clients to offer my service. At least I had that to look forward to.

"Well, well, well. Look what the cat dragged in," Nathan said in a smooth voice. Everything about him was smooth. He was like an eel.

"Well, well, well. Look what the wind blew in." I stepped inside. "Or does your hair always look like that?"

Nathan chortled. "You're not like any other maid I've ever met."

"You're not like any other rich bloke—oh, no wait, you are. How disappointing." It was nice to actually be myself, instead of biting my tongue.

"You know, I have the perfect job for you." He rubbed his hands together as his smirk transformed into a smile.

"If it involves touching you, I'm going to need bleach."

"Now you're just flirting," he said as he led the way upstairs. I followed him with trepidation. I saw Pearl's car wasn't there, but I hoped she'd return soon.

He led me to the bathroom at the end of the hall, the one that had all the blood. The blood was gone now.

"It hasn't been properly cleaned, they just rinsed it off with water until it was gone. Can you take care of it?" Nathan lingered in the doorway.

I swallowed. "Sure. No problem." Would they really have just rinsed it off with water or was he trying to mess with me?

"Excellent." He gave a wave, then walked off while whistling a tune.

He clearly wasn't concerned, which worried me. Would he really go so far as to hurt Harriet? And if she was hurt, why leave the blood? It still didn't make sense. Unless…Hmm. If I'm going to take over Harriet's wealthy clients, then I don't need Pearl and Nathan. I can spill the beans on the little argument they had, and that they were having an affair.

Which meant, I could use today to do some snooping around, especially now that Pearl wasn't around. But I had to be careful around Nathan. He seemed useless, but it didn't mean he couldn't be dangerous.

I cleaned the entire bathroom in record time and then found Nathan and Pearl's bedroom. It wasn't difficult to find since the door was open, and there were several pairs of high heels on Pearl's side of the bed.

I was closer to the staircase now, so I had to be careful and keep an ear out for Nathan. I imagined anything incriminating would be on his phone or maybe his office, but I had to try.

First I checked under the bed and even the mattress. All I found was a box of cigars, which were probably illegal, and a bunch of white pills. I put them back and just as I was heading towards the wardrobe, I heard footfalls on the staircase.

I ran and picked up my cleaning caddy, reaching the stairs just as he got to the top.

"I was just finished," I said. "What else do you need me for?"

"You could hoover downstairs." He sighed. "We'll have to find another maid, otherwise it's too much for just you."

Was that an actual nice thing he said?

"It will look bad if this place isn't spotless all the time. Besides, if you sweat too much, it will just be gross."

I raised an eyebrow. Okay, not nice at all. If this plonker worked a day in his life, he would be more familiar with sweat.

"Aren't you worried about her?"

He pursed his lips and shrugged. "It's just a stupid prank, I'm sure."

"Why would she do that?"

"Look, you just worry your pretty little head about things like hoovering and wiping."

"Does that include wiping the floor with you?" I said, clenching my fists.

I figured he'd yell at me or fire me on the spot, but instead he laughed. "I'm beginning to like you more and more."

"I'm beginning to like you less and less. Excuse me, I'll go hoover now." I attempted to walk down the stairs, but he grabbed my arm at the same time the front door opened.

He let me go instantly and looked away.

I smirked then continued on my way down the stairs as Pearl took out her earphones and checked her phone. She was in running gear and her face was sweaty.

Ha, at least someone here wasn't allergic to sweat.

"Good morning," I said.

She looked up. "Oh, hi. I'm so glad you're here." Her smile was truly lovely. She deserved way better than this poor sod she'd chosen. No amount of money in the world would make me want to be with him.

"Of course. I'm sure Harriet will be found soon. In the meantime I'm happy to work hard. I like working for you." I returned her smile.

Her face brightened even more. "Thanks, Clara. You're so sweet. I don't know what I'd do without you."

Behind me, Nathan cleared his throat. He had his hands in his pockets and walked past me to kiss his fiancé. She looked at him like he was the most precious thing in the world.

Damn, she really liked him.

"Clara was just about to hoover, weren't you?" he said as he grinned at me. Did he think he was putting me down with that remark?

"And wiping the floor," I said. "With a mop that looks good but doesn't work that well."

"Oh, dear." Pearl put her hand to her chest as if it was a drama. "Harriet never complained."

"Yeah, she had poor judgment when it came to mops." I glared at Nathan.

His lips were pressed into a thin line and if looks could kill...

I realised I'd let him know that I knew about them, but I didn't care. I was going to tell the detective the truth anyway. There was a chance that Harriet would show up and then it meant I'd lose all of her clients, but I realised I didn't want to work for someone like Nathan, although Pearl was rather sweet.

"You should probably get a new one," I said to her and then dashed off to hoover.

I DIDN'T SEE NATHAN again, much to my relief. Pearl, however, saw me out.

"You don't have to do that," I said as she followed me to my Suzuki.

"I just wanted you to know that I appreciate your hard work, especially now that Harriet is slacking off doing God knows what." We stopped at my car.

"I'm just doing what you pay me for," I said, dutifully.

She shook her head. "Nobody paid you to be nice to me, right? I think that's what I appreciate most. You seem very genuine."

I swallowed.

"Here." She handed me a card.

"What is this?" It had a name and number I didn't recognise. Darla.

"It's the number of a friend of Nathan's. She's one of the few women I actually like. I won't make you work any more just because we're down one maid. Harriet managed on her own for a few weeks. So don't worry about spreading yourself too thin. Besides, Darla only needs you twice a week." She leaned forward. "I also got you a pay rise. Pretended you were reluctant to leave me." She winked at me.

I couldn't help but laugh. "That is awesome."

"I know. Us women gotta stick together, right?"

I felt another flash of guilt as I looked back at the mansion. Still, we weren't friends. I couldn't say anything about her choice of fiancé.

"I really appreciate this." I nodded at her and then got into my car. I placed the cleaning caddy on the seat next to me and drove off while she walked back into that house.

At least I really didn't need to worry about telling on Nathan. I already had a new client. A surge of nervous energy went through me. I exhaled slowly.

It would all be okay. I just had to stay focussed.

I got home around eleven and took a quick shower before pulling on jeans and a black shirt. It was tempting to dress up, but I didn't really have anything nice and I didn't want to add to my nerves.

I did put on some extra makeup. It wasn't much, but hopefully he would notice the effort. Or was I hoping he wouldn't?

I sighed.

This was probably a bad idea. If I wanted to experience a date so badly, it would be better to just ask someone else. Someone who wasn't with the police.

Then again, Marilyn was with the police, and I'd definitely be spending a lot of time with her. Not only was it fun to hang out with the neighbourhood watch, as they really did know all the gossip, but if I gained their trust, I could even find out a little more about who I was really after.

I went downstairs, hoping I'd beat Ian to it, but he was already in the corner, right next to the double doors I'd come from.

He gave me a wave and I smiled as I hopped on over and slid into the booth.

"Hey," I said.

"Hi." He wore the same as yesterday, though a different colour shirt. His tone was light, and he looked casual enough, but his shoulders looked tense. Was it because of the search for Harriet?

"How are things going?"

"With the case or with me?" He played with his straw.

There was a pitcher with lemonade on the table and plates had already been set down. Agnes. Of course.

"Both."

"The blood belonged to Harriet," he said, carefully observing my reaction.

Great, so I was still a suspect.

Also, damn. It was really her blood.

"How awful," I said softly as I looked down. Though it still didn't make sense. Of course, just because it wasn't her blood, didn't mean she hadn't done it. It was possible.

"Since she's missing and there has been no activity from her phone or bank card, it's an official murder inquiry."

The way he said that seemed to suggest he was more in detective mode than I thought. This was definitely not going to be a fun date.

Agnes chose that time to scuttle over with two salads. She put them down.

"This is your starter. It's a tuna salad. Afterwards, you'll get some lovely toasted bread, and we'll end this lunch with a mini dessert." She wiggled her eyebrows excitedly.

I smiled at her. "Thanks, Agnes."

Ian just looked at his plate, which earned him a frown, but she didn't say anything and left our table.

"Is it possible that she could have done it herself?" I asked.

At this, he glanced up.

"She could have cut herself and smeared the blood on the walls to make it look like there had been an attack."

He leaned back, his mouth opening.

Had I said that too casually? Probably.

"Why would you think that?"

I shrugged. "Because it hadn't been cleaned. If someone killed her there, wouldn't they have gotten rid of the blood? Also, wouldn't there be more traces? They obviously got her out of that bathroom, so there would have been more blood splatters, right?"

"Not if they wrapped her body in something," he said.

Neither of us had touched our salads yet, and it was beginning to feel more and more like all work and no play.

"But why kill her in that bathroom? And again, why leave the blood?"

He tapped his fingers on the table. His grey eyes had a gleam in them as he leaned forward. I caught a whiff of his delicious aftershave and inhaled slowly, not wanting to make it look like I was inhaling his smell.

"I'll find out. It is my job to uncover secrets." His gruff voice went low again, making my spine tingle in a very pleasant way.

Also, crap. Why did this sound like a threat?

"Have you ever considered recording an audio book? You have a lovely voice."

At this, his eyes widened ever so slightly, and he glanced at my mouth. I had put on a very sincere look, mostly because I actually meant what I said. Even if I was deflecting.

"So, how long have you been single?" I added, before he could ask anything else. I had a bad feeling about whatever he meant with that remark and decided I wouldn't mention anything about Nathan and Harriet.

My survival instincts told me that it was a bad idea to bring up the fact that I'd hidden something. Maybe I could summon up the courage at the end of our little lunch.

"I—I've been single for two years now." He looked at his plate and took a bite of his salad.

I followed suit. It puts someone at ease when you mimic their body language. It was also a good idea to open up to him. It would make him more likely to open up to me.

I didn't want to tell outright lies, so I'd stick to things I was comfortable sharing.

"I've also been single for a few years, actually. I'm not the best judge of character." Also, I wasn't sure if relationships were for me. I preferred reading about the romantic versions and was simply terrified of being disappointed again. Or worse, disappointing someone else.

"Have a thing for bad guys?" Ian asked.

"Just the one," I said. "It was enough to make me wary. And what about you? What was your ex-wife like?"

He sighed as if it cost him strength to even think about her. "She was perfect, so I thought. We made each other happy. But then, it turned out she was having an affair. So, end of."

I couldn't help but be surprised at that. He seemed so cool and like he would love you with all of his heart. Why would anyone throw that away? "I'm so sorry," I said with a pained expression.

"It's why I don't like secrets. I prefer people being upfront with me." His gaze was on me again. Intent.

Oh, crap.

Chapter Eight
The Non-Date

I TOOK ANOTHER BITE of my salad so I could think of an appropriate reply. "So, she wasn't a good communicator then?"

"Not at all. I think she enjoyed sneaking around behind my back. She found it thrilling. Turns out I didn't know her at all."

"Does she live here?"

"No. Manchester. Thank goodness."

I shrugged. "Too bad. We could have egged her house."

His eyebrows rose. "You would want to do that? On a date?"

"Egg my date's ex's house? Sure." I smirked at him.

He stared back at me. There was astonishment in his eyes, but the corner of his mouth also quivered as if he was fighting a smile. "You're full of surprises, aren't you?"

"Absolutely. Have to keep you on your toes."

His smile finally broke out. "That you certainly do."

Agnes showed up to take our plates and bring our sandwiches, which we finished while continuing getting to know each other.

It was a delicate balancing act since both of us wanted to know more about the other person, so we ended up exchanging one question for an answer. It was like a tennis match of questions.

So far, I'd learned that he was born in Kent and moved here later. This is where he met his wife. He had wanted to raise a family, but of course, life had other plans. He was close to Agnes; she was like the mother he never had, though he seemed very cagey when I wanted to know more about his actual mum.

Unfortunately, it meant that he asked me about mine. I opted for the truth and told him I'd never been close to her, and that I'd only seen her recently because she was seriously ill.

To that, he seemed endearingly sympathetic, and I liked the way he looked at me with this softness that I rarely saw in anybody I grew up with. Hell, I'd never seen it in my ex.

After we finished our cheesecake, Agnes stood at our table smiling so broad she reminded me of the Cheshire cat. "How was the food?"

I groaned. "Divine. I may have to marry you."

She laughed and wagged her finger at me. "It's not me you should proposition."

Ian blushed as she said that.

"What about you? Did you enjoy the food?" she asked him.

"As always." He flashed her a charming smile that made me swoon, even if it was directed at Agnes.

She chuckled. "Go, you should find a quiet place somewhere and do whatever it is people do on dates."

Now it was my turn to blush, eliciting a raw laugh from her.

"She's actually quite wicked, isn't she?" I asked Ian.

He grinned at me. "She's the best."

I didn't doubt that for a second.

We left the pub and started taking a casual stroll. Our shoulders bumped into each other once, making me feel a flutter in my core.

What is happening?

"You said you moved around a lot, right?" He suddenly asked.

"Yeah." It was my standard answer for anyone who asked me where I was from.

"Does that mean you went to different secondary schools?"

"I did, yeah." Never long enough to make friends. Always the new girl. At least my mother had valued education. She wanted me smart. Not just street smart.

"And why move around so much?" he asked, glancing at me as we made our way past thatched cottages with lovely smelling flowers in their front gardens.

"My mother was a restless spirit," I said. I could tell him it was because of her work, but I didn't want to say too much about the kind of work she did. Somehow it felt wrong to lie. I just didn't want to, though I wasn't sure why.

Really, what is happening?

"And it was just you and your mum?"

"Yeah. What about you? Any siblings?" I wanted him to drop the topic of my mother.

"I have a half-brother and half-sister, but I'm not close to them. Nor to my dad." He had a wistful expression in his eyes and looked away.

So, if I had to guess, his dad had remarried and his mother had probably died. It was clearly not a topic he liked discussing.

"How did you end up here?"

He pressed his lips into a line and looked back at me. "This is where my mother was from."

"I see. It is a lovely place to live."

"It is. It's a village filled with odd ducks. Endearing odd ducks," he said and a smile broke out on his face. A small one, but still.

I liked that smile.

"Don't mention ducks," I said. "Marilyn might hear."

He surprised me by letting out an actual laugh.

I grinned at the sound of it. "How does she do her job with all those phobias?"

"You forget this is a village where rarely anything bad happens. She manages just fine. As long as nobody wears yellow or is a duck." He chuckled, then observed me. "You've been at the neighbourhood watch meetings then?"

"Yeah. Agnes invited me. She had me pick up Joe." I gave him a meaningful look.

"At the cemetery?" He laughed again. "I wish I could have seen that."

"I was very tempted to stake him."

"I'm glad you didn't. I would have had to arrest you," he said with a grin.

"I don't mind handcuffs." I grinned back.

There was the hint of a blush on his face, but he didn't look away.

We circled back around to the pub, to the alley where the private entrance was to my flat. The closer we got to the door, the quieter Ian became.

"I had fun," I said as I took out my key and looked at him.

He frowned slightly and the expression in his eyes was similar to when I first met him. It was reserved. Why? Had I made a mistake? Offended him? I couldn't imagine that being the case.

"Did you?" I asked with a smile.

"I just have to ask you something," he said, his rough voice lower, making it even more appealing.

"Ask me anything." My tone was casual, but in reality my heart was racing. He knew something.

He bit his bottom lip and gazed into my eyes. "I checked up on you," he said, as if discussing the weather. "And other than a Facebook page, it's very difficult to find something on you."

"Isn't that a good thing?" I tried not to look as nervous as I felt. Don't sweat, body. Sweat on the inside, or something. Or just hold it in until he's gone.

"There's always some records. For instance, your Facebook page says you went to Penwick Secondary School."

"Yeah. That was my last secondary school."

He shifted his weight. His expression was still guarded.

I could tell he was about to ask me another question, so I said: "You know, I don't appreciate you treating me like a suspect on our first date. Is your inability to let go of work a reason you don't have a girlfriend?"

By the way he winced, I could tell I'd hit a sore spot. And was right.

"It's perfectly normal to be nervous about dating, but like you said, this was just lunch. We don't have to do anything you don't want to. You don't have to find a reason not to like me." I kept my voice as neutral as possible.

He looked away and then back at me. "I have good instincts. And mine are telling me that there's something not adding up."

Damn it.

Maybe I could convince Betty to eat him.

"I'm sorry you feel that way. I still had fun, though. Thanks for having lunch with me." I leaned forward and kissed him on his cheek, inhaling his cologne.

"I'm keeping my eyes on you," he said softly. His gaze moved all over my face, and a flash of insecurity passed through me. It was a strangely intimate thing to do. I wasn't sure if anyone had ever looked at me like that. Looked that closely.

"I look forward to that." I turned around and opened the door, slipped inside and closed it quietly without looking back. Then I exhaled and realised my hands were shaking. I shook them and then dashed up the stairs. I needed to change and visit a few of Harriet's clients. I was planning on working all day, something I was now looking forward to. I needed a distraction.

Anything to not think about those light eyes and those full lips with the scar.

Perhaps he was going to use cuffs on me, but definitely not in a good way.

WHEN I LEFT FOR MY first visit to one of Harriet's clients, I went through the pub. I wanted to see Agnes and thank her again for lunch. Otherwise I risked her wanting to talk to me after I got home from work, and I had a feeling I'd need my bed.

Unfortunately, she was so busy she just waved at me. Her cheeks were red, but she still looked like she was having fun. This was clearly her happy place.

And I was the one who didn't belong here. Nor did I belong with Ian. He deserved someone much, much better than me.

I forced a smile on my face as I went outside. The first person I was going to visit lived alone and was more prone to chatting than any of the others. I needed to find some info on Harriet and fast. The sooner we solved this whole Harriet thing, the sooner Ian would be off my back.

Hopefully.

Tonight I'd tell the neighbourhood watch about Harriet's affair with Nathan, but if I had more info, that would only benefit me. If Agnes told Ian I was helping them solve this mess, he might realise I'm not trouble.

And I wasn't. Not to any of them.

Chapter Nine
The Letter

The first client I visited was Stacey Rumple, who lived alone in a large detached property. She wasn't as snooty as Nathan, and wore a simple outfit that didn't look expensive at all. It was the earrings and the two rings on her finger that gave it away. Easily worth twenty grand together.

She invited me in and proceeded to tell me half her life story. I caught the most important bits: three kids that lived in different cities, a deceased husband, two pugs and a love for horses. She owned two. She had plenty of hobbies, and listed several of them. It also meant she had very little time for cleaning and that's where I came in.

"Such a terrible shame about Harriet, isn't it?" I asked, once she finally let me get a word in.

"Oh, yes. It's gruesome, is what it is. Have they found her body yet?"

"No. Some people believe it might be a prank."

"A prank? Oh that would be awful. No, I don't think Harriet would do such a thing. She's a very friendly girl."

I nodded as if I agreed. To be honest, I just didn't know her well enough. So far, I didn't much like her for cheating with that twat Nathan.

"I wonder if she was involved in anything bad. Maybe someone wanted to hurt her," I said. Stacey was quite talkative and I wanted to get as much information as possible before getting to work. I wasn't sure if I would get the chance after my cleaning session.

"I highly doubt that. In this village." She scoffed. "This place is lovely. I only ever saw her with her boyfriend. Sometimes he picked her up. He seemed a bit possessive, but I suppose some girls like that these days." She eyed me up and down as if to accuse me too.

I nodded. Sometimes it was smarter to be quiet and let the other person fill the silence.

"She worked hard, but once, you know, I saw her try on one of my most expensive necklaces in front of the mirror. She only stared at herself for a minute, then put it back and returned to cleaning. She never stole anything. She just—well, she was just a typical girl."

"Hmm," I said, again nodding. I would never do such a thing, but I figured it proved that she had been dreaming of more.

"I hope she's alright," Stacey said.

"Me too. But in the meantime, I'll make sure your home is nice and clean."

She smiled at that. "I appreciate that. Here's the checklist."

I gasped with pleasure. "And it's laminated. I love it."

She chuckled. "Then we'll get along just fine."

AFTER I HAD CLEANED all the downstairs rooms, I was on my way to the next client. His name was Reginald Burrows and he lived on the outskirts of the village in a large estate. A woman with short brown hair opened the door for me and introduced herself as Florence Burrows, Reginald's daughter.

She told me her dad was a bit forgetful and he was resting. It meant I'd get very little out of him, but Florence was probably the one who had dealt with Harriet in the first place.

"It's a shame about Harriet, isn't it? I do hope it's all a terrible misunderstanding," I said.

We were in the middle of a tour of the place. Each room had lots of nooks and crannies and way too much stuff. It was going to be a pain to clean.

"Yes. She's missing but they found blood, right? It sounds awfully Agatha Christie-ish."

"I suppose so," I said. "What do you think happened to her?"

"How should I know? It sounds like she's dead. Maybe she slipped and Nat got rid of her body."

I wrinkled my nose at the shortened version of Nathan's name. "Really?"

"Yeah. He's a walking contrast. On the one hand, he cares about status, but on the other hand, he does dumb stuff all the time. Trust me, I went to school with him."

"He does seem rather...impetuous."

"Oh, look at you, using fancy words. Yeah, he is."

I ignored the put-down and focussed on the topic at hand. If she had gone to school with Nathan, she knew him quite well.

"Do you think he could have hurt her?"

She raised an eyebrow at me before stepping through to the kitchen. It smelt like burnt toast. "Nat would never do such a vile thing. And what for? At worst, he would shag a maid, not kill her."

Gross.

"So he's kind of a player, then?"

"Haven't you noticed? Don't worry. Give it time. Pretty women are like honey to a bear for him."

At least she thought I was pretty. Dumb, but pretty.

"Doesn't he love Pearl?" I asked.

"Oh, he doesn't love anyone but himself, that man. But don't get me wrong, he's such a dear." Her smile was as sincere as a salesman making a pitch.

"I'm sure he is. Well, I've enjoyed confabulating with you, but I should get started before I am overcome with lassitude."

She narrowed her eyes at me. "Show-off."

THE NEXT THREE CLIENTS didn't produce any new clues. They simply didn't know Harriet well enough and hadn't noticed anything suspicious. My mother would have scolded me for even thinking that anyone remotely wealthy would pay attention to a maid.

At least I'd done my best as both a member of the neighbourhood watch and as a maid. The only downside was that I was now absolutely exhausted. I drove back to the pub and ran straight to my flat. I took a shower and closed the curtains in my bedroom before falling down on my bed. A little nap wouldn't hurt.

I woke up two hours later, feeling only slightly refreshed. And starving. My stomach was making noises I didn't know it was capable of.

I changed into jeans and a long-sleeved shirt with a cute bunny on the front. Since I'd be eating at the pub, I decided to touch up my makeup. Would Ian be there?

I took the private entrance into the pub. There were a few people at the bar and at the tables, some with a late dinner. My eyes were drawn to the booth with all the neighbourhood watch members and Ian.

He met my gaze and we stared at each other for a moment until Agnes noticed me and waved me over.

"Hiya, guys," I said cheerfully.

"Ian just came over to tell us about the new Harriet clue," Agnes said.

Since Agnes was standing next to the table, I could sit down opposite Ian. I studiously avoided his gaze.

"What clue?"

"It's not necessarily a clue," Ian said while he glared at Agnes.

"Oh, come off it." She waved a hand. "It has to be. You and I both know something smells fishy, and it's not my salmon dish."

I chuckled, causing them both to look at me.

Ian's lips were curved upwards and there was a glint in his eyes.

My smile vanished. "What clue then? You're making me curious."

Joe, who was sitting next to me, still in his cape, slid over a piece of paper. It looked like a copy of a letter.

I started reading it and realised it was written by Harriet. In the letter, she said goodbye to everyone she knew and that she was leaving her life behind. She was sick of being a maid, and she wanted freedom. She ended the letter by apologising to her boyfriend.

"It's typed," I said.

"It is." Agnes looked at me expectantly. They all did.

"Well, that does seem a bit suspicious. Wouldn't you write something this personal with pen and paper?"

"Exactly." Agnes actually leaned forward so she could bang her fist on the table. "That's what we've been saying. And that," she said as she turned to Ian, "is exactly why you came to us. You don't trust it either."

Ian grinned at her. He looked very handsome when he did that. Kind of roguish.

I mentally slapped myself. I needed to stop having these thoughts.

"You see right through my nefarious plan." He winked at her.

Agnes pinched his cheek. "I always do. Now, gang. What do we make of this?"

Two new customers walked in. "Hang on, let me see what they want. Things are picking up. You guys brainstorm and come up with a plan. I'll be right there." She dashed off.

She really was one hell of a lady. I respected her a lot for running this place and starting the neighbourhood watch. She clearly cared about this community. I wish I had experienced such a feeling when I was growing up.

I could feel someone watching me. I glanced at Ian, but he turned his gaze away and scanned the others. "So, what do you guys think? Impress me with your deductive skills." There was that smirk again.

"Wait," I said. "Does this mean the case is closed?"

"Yes. It is officially closed. This was typed on her computer and her car is gone. My boss thinks the blood was a prank or a cry for attention."

"I see." So his only option was to ask us for help. It was a long shot, but at least this bunch was eager. I was honestly losing interest. It was probably very likely that she'd pranked Nathan to get back at him for not wanting to leave Pearl and was now moving on towards brighter things. Still, might as well play along.

"So she had a computer then?" Joe asked. At least he had taken out his vampire teeth. It was difficult to drink with them and he was nursing a pint of lager.

"Yes, she did. And a printer, so that checks out. The file was also still saved on the computer," Ian said.

"What was the date?" I asked.

The corner of his mouth turned upwards and he gave me a nod. "Good question. We checked that and it was written on the day before the blood was found on the walls."

"Isn't it possible then, that she left?" I asked, carefully.

"That's the thing. Her phone and bank card have been inactive ever since. Something my boss also believes is part of the prank."

"No, I don't buy that. That's a clear sign of foul play," Marilyn said. "Even if she decided to start over, you still need your phone and money. Also, her driving license and passport were still at home. So was all her other stuff."

"Could she have met someone who would have helped her?" I asked.

"If so, we have no idea who," Ian said.

"It really is a very disturbing mystery." Pavani stirred her tea and took a sip. She had a frown between her dark eyebrows. She was sitting on the same side of the booth as Marilyn and Ian.

Even if they hadn't known Harriet well, they still cared. This was their home, and they wanted to make sure it was safe.

I shifted in my seat. "Fine. Let's assume she was killed. Who had access to her computer? And who had a motive?"

"How did it go with those clients today?" Ignacius asked. He had to lean forward and peer around Joe to see me.

This was the perfect time to tell them what I knew without getting into trouble. "One of the clients knows Nathan really well. She said that he had the tendency to shag the maid."

Joe scoffed. "That scoundrel. It does not surprise me that he likes to smell other flowers while there's a beautiful one waiting for him at home."

I smiled at his choice of metaphor.

"Did he flirt with you?" Ian asked casually. Yet, his tense jaw portrayed his emotion.

"Yeah, about every time he sees me."

His mouth twitches. "And how do you respond?"

"I ask him if he wants the end of my mop in his face or up his arse."

The whole table laughed, including Ian.

"That's my girl," Joe said as he put his arm around my shoulder and squeezed.

I had never had this kind of reaction before. I mean, I found myself funny, but my mother always told me that men didn't like witty women. Pretty, not witty.

"And have you ever seen him flirt with Harriet?" Marilyn asked. She was drinking coffee and had an untouched biscuit. How anyone could not eat whatever it was Agnes put in front of them, was beyond me.

I bit my lip. This was the part where I didn't want to lie. "Well, on my first day, I saw Harriet talking to Nathan. It didn't look like it was about cleaning, but I didn't want to get involved. It was only my first day. I focussed on cleaning."

Ian took out his notebook and scribbled something. "Why didn't you tell me this before?"

I shrugged. "Like I said, I didn't want to get into trouble. Nathan pays me. This job is important to me."

Ian's eyes scanned my face, as if deciding something. I wasn't sure what. He finally nodded.

"I'm sorry," I said.

"Don't worry about it," Joe said. "You're telling us now. Combined with what that client said, it might be possible that Nathan and Harriet were an item."

"That gives three people a motive," I said. "Nathan, Pearl, and Harriet's boyfriend. What's his name?"

"Dylan."

"Another client mentioned he came across as possessive," I said.

"Maybe he knew she was cheating on him," Marilyn said. "Maybe she'd done it before. Some women are like that. Never satisfied."

"But if the boyfriend did kill her, how did her blood end up in Nathan's guest bathroom and why write that letter? And where's the body?" Ignacius asked. He was eating a slice of apple pie.

"Where does she live? Are there any good places to hide a body? I imagine it takes a lot of effort and strength to move a body and a killer wouldn't go too far, would they?"

Ian raised an eyebrow. "Thought about moving bodies a lot?"

"Only yours," I bit back.

Marilyn gasped while Ignacius chuckled.

It came out of my mouth before I could stop myself.

Ian just smiled slowly, drawing my attention to his lips.

"You can't say those things to a detective," Marilyn said, her cheeks red. "Do you want to be arrested?"

We both knew that wouldn't happen. Was she jealous of my teasing?

"That's okay," I said. "I don't mind being handcuffed."

Ignacius choked on a piece of apple pie.

"What have I missed?" Agnes asked as she popped up at our table.

Pavani laughed loudly.

Chapter Ten
Neighbourly Love

WE CONTINUED TO BRAINSTORM a few more scenarios, and reached the conclusion that Dylan, Nathan, and Pearl were our top suspects. As for an investigation plan, it ranged from stake-outs to disguising ourselves and questioning them. Since each idea easily became more ridiculous, Ian suggested we sleep on it and highlighted the importance of not doing anything stupid around potential murderers.

Although I suspected none of them would actually do any questioning. I reckoned they just liked the thrill of uncovering mysteries, but perhaps I was underestimating them.

Still, by going along with it I could get them to like me, so maybe if I came up with a good plan, they would fully accept me into their group.

"Ian, why don't you walk Clara home," Agnes said as she cleared the table. The others had scattered, probably going home. Ian and I were the last ones left and I was about to go back up and read in bed.

"Walk me home? I'm right upstairs." I raised my eyebrows. Was she still trying to set us up?

"Yes, I think that's a good idea," Ian said with a smile and exchanged a look with Agnes.

What was I missing?

"Okay," I said cautiously.

"Excellent." Ian put on his coat and directed me through the door that led to the stairs.

"Are you really going to walk me upstairs? I mean, what's the point?"

"You'll see," he said with a smirk.

Why did I have the feeling I was walking into some kind of trap?

I went up the stairs with Ian right behind me. I wasn't sure what was going on but it was making me nervous. This was making zero sense. What if he would try to kiss me? My stomach did a little flip.

We reached the two doors at the top of the stairs. I only ever saw Pavani at the pub and wondered what she was doing now. I had checked out her website and knew that she taught yoga classes as early as six AM. Which meant she was probably in bed already. I know I would have been.

I opened the door to my flat and stepped inside. "Do you want to come in?"

"Another time. Just make sure you wait two minutes before closing your curtains." There was that alluring grin again.

"Why?" This was getting weirder by the minute.

"Just do it. I'll see you." He turned around and disappeared down the stairs.

So he had walked me up just to tell me not to close my curtains yet? Why didn't he just tell me downstairs? The only reason would be that he wanted to add to the mystery. What was he trying to pull?

I closed the door, still feeling puzzled, and turned on the lights. I walked over to the window and checked my watch. Two minutes, he'd said. Clearly he wanted me to see something. Oh, no. Hang on a minute. No way. That couldn't be it.

A moment later the lights in the flat opposite me turned on and sure enough, the blinds opened to reveal a very satisfied Ian. He gave a little wave.

Great. The village's suspicious detective was living opposite me and could see into my flat.

I pointed to the right and dashed into my bedroom where I opened the door to the French balcony. Across the alley, Ian's door opened and he leaned against his balcony.

"Neighbour," he said as he tipped an imaginary hat.

I hoped I didn't look as dumb-founded as I felt. "So, that was your little surprise, huh? Why didn't you just tell me sooner?"

"Honestly, I thought you knew, but when Agnes said what she said, I realised you didn't know and I was kind of looking forward to seeing your expression." He grinned. "It was worth it."

I narrowed my eyes at him. So much for my poker face. "You're enjoying this way too much."

He chuckled. "I beg your forgiveness. It just seems quite challenging to catch you off guard."

I felt a tiny alarm bell go off. "What do you mean?"

"Your expression is always very guarded. Most of the time, it seems like you think about what you say. The surprised look on your face just now was genuine. It was nice to see." He looked down into the alley, giving me a chance to compose my-self. I didn't like what he just said. It meant that he read me bet-ter than I thought. I preferred it if he wasn't able to read me at all.

"You know," he continued, "there's this fox that usually rummages around the trash bins. I've named her Lola."

I looked down into the narrow alley, but it was empty now. "Why Lola?"

He shrugged. "It seemed to fit."

"I like foxes," I said.

"The fox usually symbolises deceit, cunning and flattery." Ian raised an eyebrow as if to suggest that that's why I liked fox-es.

"In Celtic lore the fox is a spirit guide that knows the trees the best. They are known for being clever, wise, highly adapt-able and for thinking strategically," I said.

"Is that why you like them?"

"It helps. Mostly I just think they're beautiful."

The corner of Ian's lips curved up. "That doesn't mean they're not dangerous."

"What's the matter, Detective? Don't you like a bit of dan-ger?"

He shook his head. "You know, you're not who I initially thought you were."

That means I've let my guard down too much. Why does he bring out...well, me? He is the last person I should be myself around.

"Who do you think I am, then?" I was too tempted to know what he thought of me.

But he just smiled and pushed himself away from the balcony. "Good night, neighbour."

"Good night," I said softly and watched him close the door and pull the curtain over it.

I chuckled to myself. This was just my luck, wasn't it? Just my luck.

THE NEXT MORNING, I woke up before my alarm. I got dressed and put on makeup before going into the living room to open my curtains. This was usually not the order in which I went about my morning, but I had new information now.

Ian's blinds were closed and I felt a jab of disappointment. I put on the radio in the background and turned on the kettle while I popped bread in the toaster. By the time I had buttered my toast and poured my tea, Ian's blinds were open.

There he was, in his very own kitchen, sipping his tea. His layout was the opposite of mine and his decor a lot more simple. Most of his interior was white and minimalistic. His eyes met mine and he held up his mug as if to toast me. I returned the gesture.

It wasn't too bad. During the day I was working and at night I'd close my curtains. Besides, it wasn't as if I was going to be doing anything illegal. And if I could help figure out what happened to Harriet, it would certainly make me less suspicious.

I decided to avoid eye contact with him and finished my breakfast. I got my cleaning caddy and glanced back at his flat. He wasn't there.

Okay. Good. That was probably good.

When I opened the door, there was another lunch box from Agnes. I smiled and put it in my tote bag. She really was spoiling me. I could get used to it.

My car was parked opposite the pub. As soon as I stepped out of the alley, Ian walked past the bookshop and ran right into me. He had been walking slowly, and I suspected he had been waiting for me.

"Howdy, neighbour," I said.

"Hi, neighbour. Sleep well?" he asked as he walked me to my car.

I hadn't. My thoughts kept going back to Ian and the fact that there was just an alley between us. "Well enough. You?"

"Hmm. That doesn't sound like you slept well at all. Not a guilty conscience, I hope?"

We had reached my car. I unlocked it to put my cleaning caddy in the backseat. "In my experience, people who have done bad things rarely feel guilty about it."

"In my experience, I've found the same thing. I wonder, though, how often you've come across people who have done bad things." He leaned against my car.

I knew what he was doing. He was trying to find out more about me, since he obviously felt that something wasn't adding up. He had good instincts.

I slammed the door shut and got close to him. I lowered my voice. "I'm certain that everyone has done bad things. Haven't you been bad? If not, I highly recommend it." I reached up and adjusted his tie, then ran the tie between my fingers, all the way down.

He pushed himself off the car and cleared his throat. "Thanks, err. I should probably get on with things. Busy day ahead of you?"

I had nudged him out of his comfort zone and I liked it. "Yeah, a lot of cleaning on the agenda. I'm starting with Nathan's place. I figured I could do some snooping."

Ian's lips pressed together. "Just be careful. Being part of the neighbourhood watch doesn't mean you should put yourself at risk."

I cocked my head. "Worried about me?"

"I'd be a bad detective if I wasn't." His voice was a little lower.

We stared at each other for a moment. His perfume reached my nose. I was really starting to love that scent. I couldn't help but wonder what he was thinking about while he was looking at me.

"Baaaaah."

We both jumped as Betty bleated a few feet away from us.

"Is that a thong in her mouth?" I asked, feeling queasy.

Ian sighed. "Yeah. Mrs Warren's clothing line has been filled with them ever since she got divorced. I'm pretty sure she leaves the gate open on purpose."

"Why? What does she think will happen? That a handsome bachelor stops in his tracks to pull out the underwear and asks Betty to lead her to the owner? That's a Hallmark movie waiting to happen."

Ian laughed.

I couldn't help but laugh as well.

His eyes softened. "You have a really nice laugh."

Nobody had ever said that to me. I looked away and felt my cheeks burn.

When I looked back at Ian, he was smiling at himself as if something was funny.

"I'll see you around, neighbour," he said.

"See you," I said quietly as I watched him lead Betty towards the pub. He disappeared along the side of the building, probably to return her to the garden.

I sighed. What was I going to do with him?

WHEN I ARRIVED AT NATHAN'S, the gardener let me into the house. He was a tanned man called Antonio with grey hair and twinkling eyes. He informed me, in an Italian accent, that both Pearl and Nathan weren't home. They wouldn't be home all morning.

This was music to my ears.

Pearl had left me a checklist that I went through quickly. Normally I was a lot more thorough and it felt bad to 95% it, but I wanted to snoop.

I started in Nathan's office, which I figured was the most likely place to uncover dirt. I had brought my cleaning supplies just in case someone walked in. They didn't need to know that Nathan's office wasn't on the checklist.

His office was quite tidy. He had two large bookcases, two armchairs and a desk. There was pretty much no artwork, but there were a few statuettes of half naked women in his bookcases and on his desk.

Shocker.

I started by checking the bookcase, but nothing was hidden behind the books. All the books were dusty, so there was no point checking any to see if there was anything hidden between the pages. Clearly, Nathan was not a reader. Also a shocker.

I moved on to his desk. No drawers were locked and most of the paperwork I found was actually addressed to his dad. Was it old stuff that Nathan hadn't thrown out? Or did his dad use this space? It was unlikely. As far as I understood things, Nathan lived here now. But I didn't know enough about his family to know for sure. I mean, it was strange that he'd bought his bride-to-be a fake diamond, but had expensive items in his home. I would have to ask the neighbourhood watch gang.

I did find an envelope in the back of the bottom right drawer. My heart raced as I opened it. It felt like... money. And it was. A lot of hundred pound bills. That was interesting.

I put it back and continued searching. The only other thing I found was business cards from exotic dance clubs.

Gag.

If Pearl had any secrets, they obviously wouldn't be found here. I went up to their bedroom again. Nathan had interrupted my snooping last time, but I figured if Pearl had anything to hide, I'd find it there.

Her bedside table had potpourri and a pink candle. I checked under her bed and then went over to the wardrobe. She had a lot of clothes, most of them with their tags still on.

It took some rummaging, but I found a shoe box with a big envelope. I pulled out several pictures and what looked like a written report by a PI called Jake Simms. The pictures were of Nathan and Harriet.

She knew about the affair. Pearl knew.

Chapter Eleven
Reginald

I HAD TWO MORE CLIENTS to visit today. Luckily, the clients I had taken over from Harriet didn't all need me every day. It meant I could spread out the workload. One person I had to visit again was Reginald Burrows. Which meant that I undoubtedly had to deal with his daughter Florence again. The only good thing about her was that she loved gossip. It would come in handy.

The Georgian estate that belonged to Reginald had ivy climbing along the walls and a large stable. It was a warm day and I parked my car in the corner, near the gate and next to a wheelbarrow that was placed outside the stables. I got out of my car and retrieved my cleaning caddy and tote bag.

I shut the door and looked up when there was a clanking sound. My gaze went from the wheelbarrow, to the pitchfork, to the shirtless man with the six pack who was wiping his sweaty brow.

I swallowed.

"Oh, hey. You must be the new maid," the man said.

Focus on his face.

"Yeah, I am. Name's Clara."

"I'm Dan. I'd shake your hand, but I'm kind of dirty." He grinned.

I wasn't sure if he was trying to imply anything, but I decided to play innocent, just in case.

"No worries. Good luck." I gave him a small smile and turned around.

"You look nice," he said, prompting me to turn back to him.

"Excuse me?"

"Your outfit. Very maid-like, but in a classy way. I like it."

I inhaled and pushed down the first response that came to my head. "I appreciate that." Yes, that was much better than saying anything about his current outfit. Or lack thereof.

This job didn't seem that horrible anymore. Not that Florence was that awful; I could handle her with ease. I rang the doorbell and resisted the urge to turn around. I could feel Dan's eyes on my back.

Florence opened the door. She had a black designer handbag in her hand and her eyes went from me to Dan. To be fair, he was hard to miss, even from a distance.

She cleared her throat and focussed her attention back on me. "Ah, there you are. I'm about to pop out for brunch. My father is awake and roaming about the place, but it's best to leave him alone. Like I said, his memory isn't the best. I'm sure you won't need anything. You did well yesterday. If you could continue with the downstairs rooms, that would be great. Just see how far you get in two hours and then you can go."

"I accept those tasks with alacrity. Indeed, the whole thing makes me ebullient. Just the thought of being able to contribute to the home you've envisaged—"

"Alright, alright," Florence said. "You can drop the affectation. I'm sorry, alright. I didn't mean to patronise you. Can you please stop embarrassing me any further?"

I hadn't expected her to actually apologise, nor had I realised that this was actually embarrassing to her. I was hoping to piss her off, but this was actually better. Now we could start over and hopefully have a better working relationship.

"Of course. I appreciate your apology."

She smiled at me. Her face looked years younger as she did, almost child-like. It was nice to see. "Wonderful. If you must use the restroom, use the downstairs one. I don't want you using our fancy bathrooms upstairs." With that, she trotted off.

Had I been a cartoon, steam would have come out of my ears. Just for that, I would be using the upstairs bathrooms. All of them.

Before entering, I glanced over my shoulder at Dan. Florence had walked over to chat with him. She was standing awfully close and I noticed Dan inching away from her.

I smiled to myself and went inside where it was cooler. There was a back room which functioned as a reading room. There were three large bookcases that immediately drew my attention. The sofa and poof had a similar floral print and matched the wallpaper. The small fireplace looked like it hadn't been used in a long time.

I instantly liked this room and wished I had a room like it. Such a pity that nobody seemed to be using it. I started by dusting, then hoovering, and moved clockwise through the room so I wouldn't miss any spots.

Then I brought out my all-purpose cleaner. After that I would hoover, tidy and spray the room by using half a cup of water and ten drops of cinnamon, five drops of lavender, and five drops of tea tree oil. I loved my oils and these in particular helped keep creepy crawlies at bay.

I finished wiping one of the side tables and moved on to the wooden coffee table, when I startled.

On the sofa was a man in a blue, silken bathrobe, grey trousers, and bunny slippers. He stared ahead at the empty fireplace.

This had to be Reginald, Florence's dad.

"Hi, sir. I'm Clara, the new maid," I said.

Nothing.

"I—it's nice to meet you." It felt weird to continue cleaning with him just sitting there, but I wasn't sure how unwell he was and didn't want to risk upsetting him. He wasn't harming anyone, and perhaps he was looking for company.

"I really like this room," I started. "I've always been a huge fan of reading, and I suppose it doesn't really matter where you do it, right? I'm always instantly transported to the setting of the book, but I have to say that this room is kind of perfect. I mean, it will be extra perfect when I'm done with it, but it's already quite lovely."

Great, now I was babbling. I looked at Reginald, but he just sat there, this time staring at the coffee table that looked shinier now.

"Don't tell anyone, but I'm a sucker for romance novels. I like cute romance novels, not racy ones. My favourite moments are the ones where it's clear that the main characters like each other, but they themselves don't realise it yet. Also, romance novels always have happy endings. I need to read about happy endings, because let me tell you, in real life, they don't exist." I sighed a heavy sigh and moved on to another end table. I picked up picture frames with images of what I realised was Reginald and his family. He looked so different. So happy.

I was flabbergasted when I saw a teenage Florence with a wide smile and braces. She looked like a nice girl, innocent. There was also a woman with copper hair who had her arms around both of them. It had to be his wife. Late wife? I hadn't seen her and Florence hadn't mentioned her mother.

I glanced over my shoulder at Reginald and suddenly he looked a thousand times lonelier than I felt. I carefully cleaned the frames and the table, unsure what to discuss next, so instead I just hummed a few ABBA songs.

After that, I had to hoover, so I couldn't communicate with him at all, but as soon as I was done with that, I sat down next to him on the sofa. I was sweating a little from the work I'd done so far, which meant it was the perfect time to take a break.

"Life is really just about making memories, isn't it?" I said softly. "Enough good memories so that when life finally is more about the memories you've made than about the ones you will make, they make you smile." I sighed. "So far my life isn't filled with good memories at all."

My mother had always been all I'd had left and I'd always been eager to please her. She started off her career as a thief. When she was a teen, she stole from people on the street, when she got older, and prettier, she found targets with nice homes and even nicer things inside those homes. She transitioned from petty thief to con artist, being mostly self-taught.

That's how she met my dad, but when he found out she was pregnant, he dumped her and any chance of a normal life was gone with him. And so she taught me and used me in her cons until I got old enough to realise that this was not a normal life and this was far from what I wanted for myself.

My mother had always said I was too nice, too naive. That people would eat me alive if I went out into the real world thinking the thoughts I had. To her, wanting to help people was the biggest sin of all. To her, kindness was a weapon.

She was right about me being naive. I learned the hard way that my mother was all manipulation and very little love. Although, I do believe she loves me. She just doesn't show it well.

I glanced at Reginald. "You know, I've had a lot of crappy jobs when I broke away from my mother. I wanted to do things right, even if it meant struggling. But minimum wage doesn't allow for a lot of opportunities and minimum wage jobs aren't all that fun. I have to admit, my mum's job was more thrilling, but guilt should not be part of any job. At least this time, guilt is not part of it. This will be the last thing I do for her and hopefully it will be enough." I didn't want my mum to die and even if this would be a long game, I hoped I would be in time.

"I'm sure it will be," Reginald said and turned his head to me.

My eyes widened. "W—what?"

"I said, I'm sure it will be. But your mum kind of sounds like she's a spy. Is she a spy?" He gave me an excited grin.

"You're talking," I said, and got up. I was too surprised to remain seated.

"Of course. Why wouldn't I be?"

"Your daughter said—" I started and he waved a hand.

"Oh, of course she says that. I want her to think I'm one raindrop away from drowning in madness."

I had never heard anyone put it like that. "Why?"

"Because that way she sticks around. As long as she thinks I have one foot in my grave, she'll be right here. She wants the bigger chunk of the inheritance, you see."

"Are you serious?"

He nodded vigorously. "Oh, yes. Quite fond of money, that one. In fact, it's about all she cares for."

"And you're okay with that? With manipulating her to stay with you because of money?"

"Yeah. Man, oh man, I can't wait to see the look on her face when she sees it all goes to charity. Well, I can't, unless ghosts exist." He laughed.

I shook my head. "Why is everyone in this village so weird?"

"You think *I'm* weird? There's someone who thinks he's a vampire," he said.

"I know," I said dryly.

"Anyway," he got up. "Where are you cleaning next, I'll keep you company."

I narrowed my eyes at him. "You tricked me. I've been talking to you about..." My voice trailed off as a sense of panic flooded me. What had I told him? Had I said too much?

"Calm down, girl," he said as he approached me. "You're looking very pale all of a sudden. I enjoyed your words, really. Florence never really talks to me, just complains."

I looked into his eyes and saw the loneliness again. Unfortunately, I was just as lonely, but that was why I had to stay professional. Who knew what I'd end up telling him?

"I can focus better when I'm alone. And what I said earlier, all of that was nonsense."

"Don't worry. I won't tell anyone your mother is a spy." He winked at me.

Despite myself, I smiled. "Good of you."

"You know, what you said about making memories was very nice. But what I don't think you realise is how much control you have about making those memories. It's as if memories are pictures, right? And you are the photographer. You decide what you take pictures of. If you've made crappy pictures so far, take different ones." He looked over my shoulder at the pictures I'd just cleaned. "Trust me. Life is too short."

I inhaled as I felt an unexpected lump in my throat. I'm not sure why I felt it, but a good change of topic was necessary.

"Speaking of short lives, did you hear about your former maid going missing?"

"Quite tragic, yes. She wasn't a very good maid, though."

"Why do you say that?"

"Most of her time she was chatting up Dan."

I blinked at him. "Are you serious?"

"Yes. Mind you, nothing ever happened, but they talked a lot."

She really kept busy, didn't she?

"Were they friends?"

Reginald shrugged. "I don't think they socialised outside of work. Honestly, I think she was bored with all the cleaning."

I nodded. "Did you ever notice anything else about her?"

"Like what?"

"I don't know. Anything unusual? Suspicious?"

"You mean like her mother being a spy?" His eyes twinkled.

I laughed. "She's not a spy."

"That's exactly what the daughter of a spy would say."

Reginald was beginning to grow on me. "You've got me. She's the female James Bond."

He nodded thoughtfully. "And what does that make you? Are you also a spy?"

I bit my lip. "I guess I am."

"But you don't have to be if you don't want to," Reginald said. "Nobody has to be anything they don't want to be."

"Life's too short," I said softly.

"Life's too short," he repeated.

Chapter Twelve
A Woman Not That Scorned

IT WAS LATE IN THE afternoon when I returned to the flat. I took a shower, ate a sandwich, and then googled the private eye that Pearl had hired. I wanted to talk to him about Pearl's reaction and to find out how long ago she'd found out, then I would speak with Pearl. For starters, I wanted to see if she'd lie to me, and I had to ask if she had anything to do with Harriet's disappearance.

The question was if this guy would talk to me about one of his clients. Granted, the case was over. But there was a chance he would keep his lips zipped. Of course, then the only option I had left was to go to Ian and let him do the questioning. However, if I could get this information myself, it would definitely make them all respect and trust me.

My fingers dialled the number on Jake Simms's website. I was surprised to feel a flutter of nerves. This was actually becoming exciting. It reminded me of those rare cases when we had conned rich bastards and I'd actually liked doing it. I was good at it, too. My mother had always called me a natural.

"Yeah," a gruff voice on the other line said.

"Err, hello. This is Clara McIntyre. I'm calling about a case you investigated a short while back." I mean, I assumed it had been only a short while.

"Are you a former client?" He sounded guarded.

"No."

He sighed. "Look, I'm sorry if you got outed as a cheater, but I was just doing my job. Now, excuse me."

"No, wait! I'm sorry for the confusion, but I'm also not someone you investigated. I'm calling about Pearl Pearbottom who had you investigate Nathan Weatherby. I just need to know when exactly it was and what her reaction to his infidelity was."

I held my breath.

"Why? What is this to do with you?" He sounded a smidgen more interested.

"The person Nathan was cheating with has gone missing. It's important that I know what her reaction was like and how long she's known about the affair."

"Are you police?"

Stating I was a maid suddenly seemed ridiculous. "I'm an investigator who was hired by the missing woman's parents." I should have felt bad about how easily the lie rolled off my tongue, but it didn't. This was for a good cause.

Still, a tiny part of me thought of Ian and what he'd make of this.

"Alright, then. It was only a week ago that I had told her. She was crying the whole time. She didn't seem angry, just very heartbroken. For some reason she really loved the sleazeball."

That did sound more like her. To be honest, I didn't really think of her as a murderer, but then again, I knew more than anyone that people could be very good at portraying themselves differently.

"Thanks. I guess that's all I need to know."

There was a hesitation on the other line.

"What is it?" I asked.

"There's one other thing that might interest you."

I waited.

"A few months ago, Nathan Weatherby's father hired me to look into Pearl Pearbottom. Just to find out if she had any skeletons in her closet."

"Did she?" My voice was close to being a whisper.

"No. The only thing that seems to be wrong with her is that she cares too much about money. I can't imagine her wanting to stay with someone like Nathan Weatherby for any other reason."

I sighed. "Yeah." The saddest part was that she actually cared about him. Of that I was sure. "Thanks so much for your help."

"No problem. What did you say your name was again?"

Silence.

"Miss?"

I hung up. It was a bit rude, but it was a good thing that he'd forgotten my name and that I'd called a landline. He didn't have my number, and he couldn't google my name and realise I wasn't a PI. What kind of PI didn't have a website?

His information was helpful enough. It made sense that Nathan's dad wanted to check out the girlfriend when they started dating. Even if no skeletons were found, he was probably still not a fan of her. He would want Nathan to date someone wealthy.

I rang Pearl next.

"Hello?" She picked up after the first ring.

"Hi, it's Clara. Sorry to ring you, but can you meet me at the local pub? It's kind of important." There were those nerves again, this time not from excitement. By asking her questions about Harriet, by letting her know I knew she knew about the affair, I was definitely risking my job. However, I had my share of clients now, so I wasn't too worried. In fact, I was kind of relieved to be rid of Nathan if that happened.

"Oh, okay. Is everything alright?"

"Yeah. It won't take long, I promise. Can you come now?"

"Sure. It's not like I have anything to do." She sighed. "I'll be right there."

Despite the sigh, there was a hint of excitement in her tone. She was probably just as lonely as Reginald. And me. She had snooty friends that weren't really friends, and her partner, who was also supposed to be her best friend, her confidant, was a cheating louse.

Which is why I knew she wouldn't decline my offer.

I put on some lipstick and my leather jacket. It would probably take Pearl about fifteen minutes to get here. Enough time to eat something downstairs.

The pub wasn't too crowded and I picked the table closest to the door to the house. I liked the option of a quick escape everywhere I went. Courtesy of my mother's training. *Always have a back-up lie and an exit.*

Pavani was helping Agnes out again, and she was the one who took my order while Agnes darted in and out of the kitchen.

"A lemonade and a goat's cheese sandwich."

Pavani diligently wrote it down. "How is everything going?" she asked when she was done taking my order.

"Busy cleaning. I may have a few leads, but I'll share that tonight."

"How mysterious. I like it." She grinned at me. "I look forward to hearing what you've uncovered."

I nodded at her. See, it was working. They were liking me more and more.

After a few minutes, she popped back up with my drink and sandwich. I didn't realise I was hungry until I took a bite of the sandwich. I moaned. It really was that good.

Ian walked into the pub and immediately drew my attention. A flutter of nerves arose again and I lowered my sandwich. Why did he have that effect on me? I didn't like it.

He didn't notice me and walked straight to the bar. He sat down and when Agnes popped out with a few plates and spotted him, she took a detour to kiss him on the cheek. It was endearing.

She then rushed off to bring the food to the right owners and Pavani took his order. He was ordering a pint. Was he already done with his work day? Or was this just how things were in a small village?

Either way, I was relieved he hadn't spotted me. I didn't need him to sit with me when Pearl showed up. She wouldn't know what I wanted to talk to her about, but she would be more likely to keep her mouth shut if she'd seen me talk with the detective right before.

I continued eating my sandwich, and occasionally glanced at Ian. It wasn't until the fourth time I looked his way, that his gaze met mine. A walnut nearly shot down the wrong pipe.

The hint of a smile appeared on his face, making my stomach flutter again.

He got up from his chair, but I shook my head, then glanced at the door when someone entered. It was an older man.

I relaxed and looked back at Ian again. I waved him away and put my finger to my lip, hoping that it was clear enough that I needed him to stay away and that I was a woman with a mission.

He frowned, but sat back at the bar. He had his body turned sideways, though, so that he could easily look at me.

I finished my sandwich just in time, because Pearl came bouncing in and waved a manicured hand at me just as Pavani collected my empty plate.

"Want a drink?" she asked Pearl.

"Iced tea, please." She had on a lot of makeup, but at least she was smiling. It was a genuine smile and she seemed pleased to see me.

I squirmed in my seat, uncomfortable about the conversation we were about to have. "Thanks for coming."

"No worries. Is everything okay? Please don't tell me you're going to quit. I'll give you a bonus for all the hard work you're doing, but I do rather like having you around. You're a good maid and you're nice."

I wasn't sure how she got that. I mean, we hadn't talked that much, had we?

"I don't want to quit, no. Do you know that I'm part of the neighbourhood watch?"

She raised her eyebrows. "Err, no. Is that significant? Doesn't that just mean you keep an eye on things and text the other people in the group gossip?"

I managed a smile. "In a way." My smile faded. "In this case, it means that we've been looking into Harriet's disappearance. The group found out that you hired Jake Simms a week ago." I remained quiet, because I wanted her to fill in the rest. The less I talked, the better.

The corner of her mouth turned downwards. "I see." Her expression became cold and I instinctively pulled my glass towards me. Just in case she was inclined to throw it in my face.

Pavani showed up to hand her her iced tea.

Crap.

She was now armed and dangerous.

"I'm sorry," I said, going for the soft approach. "You must be terribly upset. You don't deserve what he did to you."

She closed her eyes and when she opened them, tears spilled over her blushed cheeks.

Oh, no. Crying was worse. Way worse. I would have preferred her throwing her drink in my face.

I inhaled and reached out for her hand.

She grabbed it and smiled through her tears. "You're very sweet." She wiped her face with her other hand. "I know what you must be thinking, but I don't...I didn't do anything to Harriet. I didn't want to. When she had become distant with me, I suspected something was going on between her and Nathan. When I got the proof that she was, I decided that it was simply something Nathan needed. An adventure. He is easily bored. I accepted that this was the situation. When you found that blood... I mean, it's obviously a cry for attention. I know

Nathan would never go for Harriet in the long run. Men like him don't go for maids." She looked up at me. "No offense."

"None taken. I know that's true."

"I figured I'd just keep things very professional with Harriet. And it's also the reason I wanted a second maid. I just didn't like the idea of leaving when she was home alone with him, you know?"

I leaned forward. "Why did you feel you needed to accept it, though? Do you not realise you deserve so much better?" I had to say it.

She laughed, but it sounded wry. "That's the thing. I don't think I deserve better. It's very difficult to go for something you think you don't deserve."

I glanced at Ian, who was staring at us. I quickly looked away.

"I guess so," I said.

"Well, that's how it is. But I thank you for saying those kind words." She took a few swigs of her drink and then got up. "Look, I really didn't hurt that Harriet and I truly believe nobody did." She put some money on the table.

"Oh, no—"

"Thanks for hanging out with me." She turned on her heels and strolled out of the pub, her hips swaying.

How she could classify that as hanging out was beyond me. The fact that she wasn't angry either indicated she truly believed what she'd said. That Harriet wasn't in any danger. And I was beginning to think that maybe that was true.

Ian slid into the booth opposite me. "Want to share what that was about?"

I sat up straighter. "Just a bit of sleuthing."

"And what did you uncover, Nancy Drew?"

"Pearl hired a PI to spy on Nathan and had proof that Nathan was having an affair with Harriet."

I would have loved to take a picture of Ian's expression. Pure surprise was something I hadn't been privileged to witness before.

"She said that she had accepted that he wanted to have an affair and said that's why she hired me." I frowned. "Wait, that sounded wrong."

Ian grimaced. "Wild plans with Nathan?"

I made a face. "I meant that she didn't want Harriet to be alone with Nathan whenever she had to leave."

"I got it. And do you think she's telling the truth? That she wasn't angry enough to hurt her?"

I shrugged. "People can wear any mask they want, but no, I don't think she's lying."

He tilted his head as his eyes scrutinised my face. I didn't like that. It made me feel naked and vulnerable.

"There may be people who wear masks, but there are also plenty who don't." His voice was extra low.

I simply smiled. "Is this helpful?"

He leaned back. "Actually, yes. This was good work. I'll still go and talk to her, but it's a lead. You didn't do anything illegal to get this information?"

"Nope. I was just cleaning. I can't help what I come across." I winked at him.

Ian smiled back. "That's what I thought. Good work."

A peculiar feeling settled in my chest at the compliment and my expression fell.

"Are you okay?" He frowned.

"Yeah. Yeah. I have to go." See, this was why exits were handy. All I had to do was get up and take the three steps to the door. I closed the door behind me and felt like I could breathe again.

I definitely needed an exit whenever I was near Ian.

Chapter Thirteen
Maid, Interrupted

I STAYED UP IN MY FLAT until my stomach rumbled again around dinner time. At the thought of seeing Ian again I felt nervous. I was not the type to get nervous over a guy. Right? I was fierce and independent.

My stomach rumbled again.

Also, I was very hungry.

I put on some more makeup. Since I didn't like to wear much while working, I figured I might as well go all out after work. It had nothing to do with Ian. Nothing.

The vicar was at one of the tables with Joe. I smiled at the sight of them, then immediately felt bad. I shouldn't get attached to them. I was going to be out of here as soon as I could and they'd never hear from me again.

Ignacius spotted me and waved me over. I hurried to their table and sat down. "How are my favourite lads?" I asked them.

At this, Ignacius chuckled and Joe's eyes twinkled.

"Are we your favourites, yes?" Joe asked. "I feel special."

"You should," I said.

"Usually when a woman says things like that, it means she's done something wrong," Ignacius said. "Did you do something bad?"

I swallow. "What could I have possibly done?"

He shrugged. "You're right. This pertains to spouses, I reckon."

"Not mine," Joe said. "If anyone always got into trouble, it was me. Not on purpose, and not seriously. Usually she yelled at me because I dragged mud into the cottage, or because I had promised neighbours we'd cook them a meal. Somehow they'd always be the neighbours my wife hated. And then she'd have to cook them a delicious meal and dessert." He laughed. "Mind you, she was as polite as a kitten to them, but then when they were gone, she wouldn't speak to me all night."

I smiled. "It still must have been nice to make memories like that. Memories you could laugh about later on."

"Absolutely. Plus, I always made it up to her. I gave her the best foot rubs ever."

"Ah, Ian," Ignacius suddenly said. "Why don't you join us?"

"Don't mind if I do," Ian said as he looked at me, then slid into the booth next to me, forcing me to move over to the window.

Great, I was officially boxed in. No exit route.

"What were you guys talking about?" he asked.

"About my wife," Joe said.

Ian raised his eyebrows. "You don't talk about her often."

"Because everyone knew her so well. But our girl here doesn't. I'm going to pull out all the stories." He winked at me.

I couldn't contain my grin. "I would love that."

"Our girl, huh?" Ian said as he smiled at me. "I like that."

I narrowed my eyes at him. "Does that make you *our* detective?"

"Oh, yes. It does," Ignacius chimed in.

Ian glanced at him. "Well, I suppose it does, since it is my job to protect you all."

"I'll remember that when I've had a terrifying nightmare," I said, causing Ignacius to nearly choke on his next bite of spaghetti.

This elicited another smile from Ian, this one more wicked than usual. I also liked the glint in his eyes. That was new.

Whatever he thought of me, it couldn't be too bad since he was joking around with me. Perhaps he thought of me more as a victim with a new identity rather than a former criminal.

My mouth felt dry as a fresh wave of guilt washed over me. If guilt was liquid, I'd be soaked to the bone.

I looked away from Ian, but I could still feel his gaze on me. Why did he have to be so perceptive?

I would just have to work harder on my poker face. I smiled at Joe. "What about you, Ignacius? Ever married?"

"Three times," he said as he held up four fingers.

Uhm.

Agnes showed up at our table. "Two new hungry patrons. Did you come in together?" She regarded Ian and me with a sprinkle of hope.

"No," I said quickly. "Can I get fish and cheesy chips with gravy?"

Ian glanced at me. "Same for me. Thank you."

"Well, just because you didn't come in together, doesn't mean you won't leave together." She winked at me.

I blushed.

Again, Ignacius coughed up his latest bite while Joe patted him on his back.

Ian simply chuckled and placed his arm on the back of the seat and turned to me.

Oh, boy. Was it getting warmer in here?

His aftershave smelt divine. I wanted to ignore him, but felt compelled to look into his all-seeing eyes.

"So, you really dashed off to your flat this afternoon, only to return an hour later?" he asked.

"Yeah."

"Why did you not stay?"

"What would I have done here?" I retorted.

He raised one eyebrow. "Stay and chat with me, for example." He leaned closer. "Unless that makes you nervous."

Why was there no exit? Would it be frowned upon if I jumped through the window?

"I had to read."

"Read?"

"Yes, I had the desperate urge to read one of my books, which was infinitely more enjoyable than spending time with you."

Both Joe and Ignacius had stilled and were following this conversation with interest.

Ian chuckled. "That's funny because as I recall you had quite a good time during our non-date."

"Except for when you basically accused me of who knows what."

"If you have nothing to hide, then why wouldn't you want to spend time with me?"

"Maybe you're boring," I said without thinking.

At this, Ian flinched and his expression filled with pain. Instinctively, I knew this was something someone had accused him of before. Of course. His ex wife. I had hit the mother of all sore spots.

Ian removed his arm and turned away from me. "I—I think I'll eat at the bar," he said and started to move away.

It would have been so easy. With these three words I could have potentially pushed him away. He would have no more interest in me and I wouldn't have to worry about getting attached or getting found out, or both. But somehow, the look in his eyes, the hurt, it was unbearable.

I clasped his sleeve and pulled him back. "I'm sorry. I promise you on my life that I didn't mean that. I take it back, okay?"

He just stared at me.

I put my hand on his cheek and kissed his other one. "I'm so sorry. Please forgive me."

I heard one of the men gasp. Probably Ignacius.

Ian's gaze darted from my lips to my eyes. He nodded.

Relief surged through me as I let go of his sleeve and relaxed in my seat. Joe and Ignacius were still staring at us.

"Your dinners are getting cold," I said flatly.

I was just glad Agnes hadn't seen the kiss, though I was certain the whole neighbourhood watch would learn of our exchange before the night was over.

I was struggling to think of something to say to change the atmosphere when Marilyn came over. "Hi, guys. May I join you?"

"Sure," Ian said and moved closer to me.

I scooted as close to the window as I could as Marilyn joined us on our side of the booth. Ian's thigh was touching mine and we exchanged a glance.

Soon, we had our food and I was happy to be able to focus on something, or, at least, pretend to. I was still very aware of Ian, and I liked sitting this close to him. It made me feel safe. Which in turn made me feel silly. I had always managed to take care of myself. But perhaps being taken care of and being safe were different things.

I had known my ex, Rod, since I was fifteen. He helped my mum with some cons. He was extremely good with cars and safes. He also had a degree in art, even if he didn't look like it. He kind of looked like a hoodlum at that age. It wasn't until he was older that he started to dress better. My mum was a massive fan of his. In hindsight, she had a hand in us getting together, but I was still genuinely in love with him. Or at least, that's what I'd thought. I had never felt anything as strong as what I was feeling right now and Ian and I hadn't even done anything romantic.

My mother had taught me that being in love was a feeling of liking someone and wanting to spend time with them and that any other notions were made up things from films. Now I wasn't so sure.

Perhaps it was best if I stayed away from Ian. Who lived across from me. And who was sitting next to me and probably would many more times to come.

I just had to deal with whatever this was. It was probably just me getting carried away with the comfy vibe of this village. It was making me wish for things I would never have.

AFTER DINNER, THE REST of the neighbourhood watch showed up, and Ian seemed to want to stay for it. Perhaps because his investigation was put on the back burner ever since they found Harriet's letter. I wondered what he did in his free time. Did he hang out here? Most of the residents seemed to come here, even if the neighbourhood watch consisted of the hardcore regulars.

Agnes and Pavani made sure we were all provided with tea, but before we could start, a pale, heavy woman burst through the door. She was dressed in a beautiful pink dress that matched her cheeks. She seemed to be in her forties.

"Oh, thank goodness you're here, Detective Ian," she said with all the drama of a soap opera actress.

"I told you to call me Ian," he murmured in response while the others didn't seem too affected by the woman's panicked energy.

I'm pretty sure Joe rolled his eyes as soon as she had opened her mouth.

"What is it this time?" Marilyn asked, the only one who actually seemed to want to help. She even sounded a bit excited.

Ian took a sip of his tea.

"It's Precious. She's gotten out and I fear for her life. There was a raccoon sniffing around my garbage cans. What if he kills her?"

I leaned forward. "Who is Precious?"

She narrowed her eyes at me as if she only just spotted me and didn't like what she saw. "Who are you?"

"I'm Clara," I started, but was cut off.

"Of course. The new maid. You must be happy you've got more work now that Harriet's gone," she said.

"Doris," Pavani said in a sharp tone.

Ian cleared his throat. "There is no need for that."

I raised my eyebrow at that. He was suspicious of me and yet he stood up for me.

"What? I'm just saying, she's new. How do you all know you can trust her?"

"Good point," I said.

They all looked at me.

"What? It's a good point. I might be wholly untrustworthy and a despicable human being."

Agnes sighed loud enough for all of us to hear. "You're not. And Doris, you can't just talk to her like that because she's new here. Now, we know how much you care for Precious and we will all help you find her."

"Again, who is Precious?" I asked.

TEN MINUTES LATER, we had paired up and spread out around Doris's cottage, fanning out towards the edge of the village. Ian had paired up with me, or more accurately, Agnes had paired us. Big surprise.

We'd both turned on the flashlight on our smartphones. It was quiet save for the occasional dog walker or people strolling to or from the pub.

"I can't believe Doris got the whole neighbourhood watch to actually search for an escaped hamster," I said.

"And not the for the first time," Ian added. "She lets Precious roam around the garden in one of those hamster balls but she escapes on a regular basis, causing her to panic and let us do all the work."

"Yeah, I think it's more pretend panic with the goal to make us do the work. I say we buy her a new hamster and go back to the pub."

Ian chuckled. "Not a fan of rodents or just not a fan of hanging out with me because I'm that boring?"

I looked at him and his smile indicated he wasn't actually upset with me. Not anymore, anyway. "I really am sorry about saying that. I didn't mean it."

He shrugged. "Even if you did—"

"But I don't," I said a little louder than I had intended. "I find you very interesting and I don't like that anyone has made you feel like you aren't."

Ian slowed down to a halt and faced me. "Really?" His eyes searched my face. "And what makes you think anyone had?"

Oh, right. He hadn't actually said that. "You seem to be able to take a joke, so your reaction indicated that someone had used that to hurt you. I'm guessing your ex wife?"

"You're sharper than you let on. I should remember that."

I felt my cheeks burn. Damn. Why do I keep showing him parts of the real me?

"I—I just have good intuition."

"Maybe you should become a detective, then." He continued walking.

"I don't think I'd handle dead bodies very well."

"I should hope not. But you don't really have to. The coroner and CSU deal with that aspect." He bent down and shone his light under one of the bushes at the side of the road that led to the next cottage.

"Why'd you become a detective?" I asked.

"I like solving mysteries." He walked a few paces, then sighed and came to a stop. "No, that's not really it. I guess I did it because of my mother. She was killed when I was a baby."

Chapter Fourteen
Precious

I GASPED AT THIS INFORMATION. How awful.

"It has always been my goal to solve that murder, since nobody else did." He glanced at me. "You must think I'm very naive." He started walking very slowly and I matched his pace.

"No, not at all. I'd do the exact same thing."

"You would?"

"Oh, yeah. I'd do everything I could to nail that monster. But it must not be easy since it was so long ago and things were different. Is there much evidence?"

We stopped walking again. This wasn't really something you discussed while looking for a hamster.

"No. She was killed in our home, while I was upstairs in the crib and my father was at work. It happened in broad daylight and nobody saw a thing. There was a black fibre on her dress, but that was all they found."

"H—how—I mean, if you don't mind me ask—"

"She was strangled." He swallowed and couldn't say it while making eye contact.

I touched his arm. "I'm so sorry. Look, don't feel pressured. It's not your job to solve it. And your mother, wherever she is, is very proud of you regardless of whether you solve her murder or not."

He blinked and I was certain I saw his eyes moisten. He leaned forward and placed his hand behind my neck, pulling my face closer to his. His lips touched my forehead gently before he let go again. "Let's go find this hamster."

I exhaled slowly as he moved away from me. He was a very strong person who carried a lot of pain. It was very bad that I wanted to take some of that pain away from him.

I had a mission myself. He was doing something for his mother, and I was doing something for mine.

We reached one of Doris's neighbours with a similar cottage to hers. It had a thatched roof and a few garden gnomes by the green door. One of the gnomes showed his bum. There were a lot of bushes in front of the low, white gate around the small front garden.

"These cottages are really nice," I said to Ian.

"Aren't they? Much better than a flat."

"Why didn't you choose a nice cottage then? Are they that expensive?"

Ian leaned forward and checked under the bushes. "I lived in one of them with my ex-wife. It's really the sort of place for a family, at least in my opinion. Unfortunately, as you know, life had other plans."

That damn ex-wife of his was a fool.

There was a rustling from one of the bushes in front of the gate.

"Did you hear that?" I asked, as I shone my phone in the direction of the noise.

"Yes, I did," Ian whispered.

We both inched closer to the bush. Our heads were nearly touching as we bent forward to peer through the leaves and twigs.

Out shot something bright orange as if with light speed. I gasped and lost my balance, falling onto my butt.

Ian chuckled as he helped me up.

"Is that the—how is it so fast?" My eyes followed the zig-zagging hamster ball as it sped across the road.

"That's Precious all right." When Ian realised he was still holding my hand, he stared at me for two seconds before dropping it. "We should go catch her."

But I was already getting ready. "Leave it to me," I said. I put my phone in my pocket, lifted up my socks and got into a runner's position. Three. Two. One.

"What are y—"

I darted forward, my eyes still on the hamster in her bright orange ball as she zoomed across the road without a care in the world. She'd clearly had a taste of freedom and probably also wanted to get away from Doris, but Precious had made me fall, so I wanted to get the little rascal.

I had no idea how good her vision was, but she seemed to notice my approach and attempted to roll towards the side of the road and into the grass. I intercepted her, and threw myself on the ball with the grace of a drunk hippo.

With a thud, I landed on the asphalt. Had I gotten it? I checked my arms and there it was. A bright orange ball with a fluffy hamster inside. Her tiny whiskers were twitching with dismay.

"Ha, gotcha!" I couldn't hide the triumph from my voice and behind me Ian laughed as he approached us.

"I have never seen anyone do a dive like that unless it was for a rugby ball." He wiped his eyes as if he was crying with laughter.

I narrowed my eyes at him as I got up. Precious was in my hands and I could practically feel her glaring at me from inside the ball.

"It wasn't that funny."

"Yes, it was. I promise you it was. My only regret is that I didn't take a picture."

I handed him the hamster in its round trap. "I'm going back to the pub."

"Oh, no, no, no. We'll go and bring Precious back together. Doris has the tendency to reward me whenever I return the hamster—somehow it's usually me that finds her."

"Afraid of a middle-aged lady?" I crossed my arms.

"Not afraid. I'm just very polite, that's all."

"Yeah, and she takes advantage of that, I'm sure. Okay, let's go. I guess I'll protect you."

Ian laughed.

We rang Doris's doorbell a moment later. Her cottage looked well kept on the outside and there was a small pond with a bench in her front garden. I could just imagine sitting there in the morning with a cup of tea. Do these people know how blessed they are?

"Ah, you found her," Doris said by way of greeting. She leaned towards Ian who was holding Precious as if she was going to kiss him.

"Actually," he said as he pushed Precious into my hands, "Clara found him. She did a really good job at catching her."

She hesitated as she stared at me. "Thanks," she said primly and then yanked the hamster ball out of my hands.

Precious had her paws up against the ball as if she was begging us to take her back. Perhaps I had to stage a rescue at some point.

"No problem. We have to get back to the pub. Our dinner is waiting for us." I pulled on Ian's sleeve and turned around.

"Hang on," Doris said. "Are you looking into that Harriet business?" She directed her question to Ian.

"There's not much to look into. She left a goodbye note," he answered.

"Yeah, well. I literally bumped into her a few days ago and she dropped her bag." She eyed Ian as if that was enough information right there.

"Alright," Ian said hesitantly.

She waited.

Okay, this woman clearly liked attention. "What is so significant about that?" I asked, taking the bait.

She ignored me as she maintained eye contact with Ian. "A lot of money fell out. A whole stack of paper money."

Ian and I exchanged a look.

"Anyway, thanks for returning Precious to me. It is just so quiet without her," she started and I knew this was going to be a long monologue.

"Glad to have helped. Bye bye," I said loudly, interrupting her before she could say more. I grabbed Ian's arm and pulled him away. It was about time I got my cheesy chips with gravy.

Since Ian texted everyone as soon as we found Precious, Joe and Ignacius were already back at the table. Agnes set our plates down as soon as we sat down.

"I've kept this warm for you. Enjoy," she said, then had to dash off straight away. This dinner rush had her cheeks flushed.

"Who is helping her tonight?" I asked.

Ignacius and Joe had finished their dinner so they were nursing beers.

"Pavani and Marilyn are," Joe said as he studied a ketchup stain on his cape. It kind of looked like blood. Ha.

I wondered how Marilyn would handle any kind of dish with yellow food on it. Probably not well. How would she handle roasted duck? I chuckled to myself.

"Something funny?" Ian asked.

I shook my head. "Inside joke with myself."

He grinned and leaned towards me. "Marilyn and duck?"

"Exactly!" I laughed.

Wrinkles formed around Ian's eyes as he laughed as well.

"What are you two giggling about?" Ignacius asked. "We feel very left out." His lips turned upwards, though.

"Inside joke," Ian and I said simultaneously. We glanced at each other and grinned.

"Speaking of jokes," Joe said, as he started telling us a Betty story that involved a shoe, an inebriated bride, and a coach full of tourists. He himself laughed so hard, his fake teeth fell out.

As soon as the pub quieted down, Agnes joined our table. "Have I missed anything? Why are you guys chatting and laughing? We should discuss the case." Marilyn was still helping out in the background.

"Yes, ma'am," Joe said as he saluted her with a cheeky wink.

"Did you find out anything new when cleaning?" Agnes asked.

All eyes were on me. I hadn't gotten a chance to tell them about Pearl yet and it seemed Ian hadn't either, so I filled them in.

"Look at you, investigating on your own," Agnes said with a smile.

"That was very brave of you," Pavani added.

I shrugged. "Not really. I met Pearl in a public place."

"Even so, you showed some real initiative," Ignacius said before taking a sip of his tea.

"I—I guess. Thanks." They seemed to regard me with some level of respect. It was good, but also strange. What I had done wasn't special at all. I could do much more.

"Does this mean she's a suspect now?" Agnes asked Ian.

Ian didn't indicate I had already told him this. "We still need more than this. We need proof or a confession. Preferably both."

"I did find out Harriet sometimes talks to one of the workers at Reginald's estate. His name is Dan."

"Oh, Dan," Pavani said with a sigh. "If I was lightyears younger, I'd go for him."

I chuckled at that.

Ian shifted in his seat. "You saw Dan?"

"I did." Why did he seem uncomfortable?

"Did he have his shirt off?" Agnes asked, eyes narrowed.

I couldn't help but smile at the mere thought. "He did."

Ian stared at me.

"What?"

"Nothing," he grumbled.

"Okay, look," Agnes said as she leaned forward. "He may have nice abs, but there's nothing else that makes him special.

Alright, that's mean. He is a nice guy—" she glanced at Ian who made eye contact with her, "—but not even that nice."

Oh, I got it. Ian was jealous and Agnes was worried I might find someone more interesting. I could have some fun with this.

"His abs weren't just nice. They were divine. Dare I say godlike, even?" I pretended to think while everyone turned to me. "Yeah, I dare say that. Definitely godlike."

Pavani giggled.

Ian's jaw was locked. He was definitely not happy and both Joe and Ignacious seemed somewhat shocked that I just came right out and said that.

"And he was also sweating, so his skin was glis—" I started, ready for another round.

"Okay, we get it," Ian said with an edge. "We get it." He took a swig of his tea and then immediately clasped his hand over his mouth as if he had burned his tongue.

"But I did find out that Harriet and Dan talked a lot. They seemed to be buddies, sort of. Maybe she told him something that can help us find out what happened?"

This certainly piqued Ian's interest. "Hmm. Okay, leave it to me. I'll have a chinwag with him."

The meeting soon unravelled, mostly because we didn't really have anything new to discuss about the case. All we could do was keep our eyes and ears open.

Ian still had me boxed in and he didn't make any indication he was moving. Neither did I. Joe and Ignacius were the last of our group to leave. Agnes was in the kitchen now that only a handful of people were left in the pub.

I stretched myself, as my back was beginning to get sore. It was definitely time for bed. "Alright, I guess I'll be going," I said.

Ian tapped his fingers on the table, not looking at me.

"Are you going to move?" I asked.

"Are you really attracted to Dan?" he asked, still not making eye contact.

Wow. Did he really care that much? Perhaps I had underestimated how much he liked me. He really seemed bothered by this Dan thing. I could use this. I should use this. Right?

"I can't deny that I'm attracted to him," I said, thinking back to Dan's alluring physique.

Ian stopped his tapping.

He was asking the wrong question here, but that was a good thing. I was getting way too close to him.

"Anyway, I should go now." I started scooting his way, but since he still didn't move, I just ended up closer to him.

I hadn't expected him to look into my eyes, our faces quite close. "Do you like him?"

"Not one bit," I said automatically. Damn. I really needed to stop telling the truth. It was probably because of how close we were sitting. It caught me off guard. That was all.

"I really need to go now. Could you move?" I managed to keep my expression neutral and my voice steady.

"Is that what you want?"

That question made even my eyebrows sweat. What was he really asking me?

"Yes, that's what I want," I said.

He moved and I escaped to my flat, feeling like I was starting to fail my mission.

Chapter Fifteen
Harriet

I GOT UP EARLIER THAT morning because I didn't want to risk running into Ian. It was best to keep things as civil but distant as possible. My first client of the day was Pearl. I wasn't particularly looking forward to going over there, but that had everything to do with Nathan.

I parked my car and got out. The gardener was there again as well and he let me in before I could even ring the doorbell. He was all smiles, nearly bowing as he let me in.

I chuckled.

So far, Pearl had always told me what needed to be done, which meant I had to find her in this big mansion. It would actually be easier to ring the doorbell. But then I heard it.

Pearl's and Nathan's voices. They didn't sound happy.

Could it be about Harriet?

I followed their voices to Nathan's office. It gave me a flashback to when I'd overheard him talking to Harriet.

Could she be breaking up with him? I hoped so for her sake.

"Why are you lying to me?" Pearl asked him.

I stayed out of sight because I wanted to eavesdrop. Well, I didn't feel comfortable doing it, but if it was related to what was going on with my missing colleague, I had to know.

"I'm not lying, I just bumped into my car door," Nathan said.

"With your eye? I don't think so. Who punched you?" Pearl's voice actually sounded firm. I liked it.

"Nothing, I told you. You're being overprotective. Sweetheart, come on." His voice had gone all soft and gooey and he was clearly putting the moves on her. A distraction.

This was interesting. Someone had punched him and he didn't want her to know who. Could it be Harriet's boyfriend? Or did Nathan have other enemies?

"No," Pearl said loudly. "There have already been too many lies between us. I refuse to accept more. We speak the truth or it's over."

I nearly gasped. She was finally standing up for herself.

Nathan cleared his throat. "You're right." He suddenly sounded more mature as he said that. And less sleezy.

"Go on. I won't judge you. Just tell me what happened." Pearl's voice was gentle now.

"Fine. I've been playing poker with a couple of shady people. The stakes were pretty high, but I lost a lot of money in the past few...err, well years." He cleared his throat again.

"How much?"

"A lot. I don't even know the exact number, but it's a lot. I've paid off some by getting rid of some of the stuff in this place, but it's not enough yet and I can't sell too much or my dad will throw a fit. Lots of these are heirlooms, you know?

Anyway, every now and then this guy's men threaten me. That's all."

"That's all? That's awful. Baby, why didn't you tell me this sooner?"

"I was embarrassed, okay? I just—it's my mess. I have to fix it myself. And I will. Just don't worry."

"I'll get a job. I can help you," Pearl said.

She was way too good for him.

"No, of course not. It would not be right if my fiancée did that. I'll fix it, just stay out of it and for crying out loud, don't tell anyone."

Come on, ask the name of the guy who he's indebted to.

"Okay, I won't. It will be okay, baby." Pearl said and then there was a moment of silence. They were probably hugging or kissing.

Gross.

I wish I knew who was in charge of the underground poker games. I could probably find out. Quietly, I returned to the entrance and called out Pearl's name.

"The gardener let me in!" I shouted. "Hello?"

Pearl came out to greet me. "There you are, nice and early. I appreciate your eagerness." She smiled, though I knew she had to be worried about Nathan.

"I've actually made you a list," she said. "Follow me." There was a storage area with cleaning supplies and on the inside she had taped a laminated schedule for me. Now I could see what I had to do whenever I was here. I liked it. Especially if it meant I didn't need to speak with Nathan.

"Thank you so much," I said. "I'll get started right away."

"Alright, I'll have a cup of tea ready when you're done."

I blinked at her. She had never done that before. She probably needed someone to talk to.

"I look forward to it." I smiled at her and then got to work on the staircase. It wasn't long before Nathan left. He was vague to Pearl about where he was going and I could tell she worried even more now, but she left me to do my cleaning.

I worked a bit faster than usual, but that was because Nathan's office was on my to-do list and now that I knew he owed someone bad a debt, I wanted to see if I could find some kind of proof of that.

I had to be careful because Pearl was home, but I bent down behind his desk and tried to find his diary. I wanted to know if he had written down any appointments or names that could tell me where he had these games.

There was a big black diary in one of his drawers but it was completely empty. He probably kept all his appointments on his iPhone. I tried to look for well-hidden papers but there was nothing. I had the feeling this office was more for show. Nathan wasn't the type to meticulously keep track of things. Besides, it sounded like his dad owned this place. Still, I had hoped now that I was searching for something particular that I would find it.

I continued cleaning and then went into the kitchen, hoping that Pearl could help me get even more clues. Of course, Nathan's debt could have nothing to do with Harriet, but I needed to know as much as possible, even if it was just to pass along at the neighbourhood watch meeting.

Pearl, as promised, had put on the kettle and poured us both a cup of tea after I walked in. I was sweating a little, but she didn't seem to mind. We sat down at the white kitchen island. It was lunchtime and I took out my lunch box with the chicken sandwich that Agnes had made for me.

"So, everything okay?" I asked.

"Is it that obvious?" Pearl gave me a weak smile. "I just always thought I'd be happy at this point in my life, you know?"

"Being an adult, you mean? Or being engaged?"

"Both, I suppose. But especially engaged. He's wealthy, charming, and a great kisser, but things aren't perfect."

I fought down the nausea caused by her descriptions of Nathan and nodded sympathetically. She had one elbow on the marble counter and her hand on her tea mug. I mimicked her body language to put her at ease.

"I see," I said softly.

Pearl sighed. "Nathan apparently has money troubles. Please don't tell anyone, but I just find it so easy to talk to you. I trust you."

I put my hand on her arm. "You can tell me anything." Technically it was not a lie, but I hated how easily the things my mother taught me bubbled up.

"I think Nathan got involved with some bad people and now he owes them money. He doesn't want me to get a job, but I want to help him. Do you know of any jobs that I can take on?" She looked at me with wide eyes.

"Are you sure that's what you want?" I asked, knowing her well enough already to know that it was. She had tied herself to Nathan and wasn't going to cut the rope anytime soon.

"Of course. I love him. I told you that. He's not perfect, I know. But I'm lucky to have him and I want to help him. He would do the same for me."

I nearly laughed, but managed to contain myself. Besides, I wasn't here to help her or be her friend.

"Actually, I do know of someone who needs a bartender. Her name is Agnes and she's lovely."

"Wait, at the pub we met, right?" Pearl sounded perkier already.

"Yes, that's right."

She clasped my hand. "That would be perfect. Nathan is usually out in the evening, so he won't even know I'm not there."

That was kind of sad.

"Wonderful," I said.

IN THE AFTERNOON I went over to Stacey Rumple, whose pugs followed me around all day while she was out riding her horse. I secretly loved it and occasionally played with them. I had always wanted pets. In fact, I had begged my mother's ears off. She had gotten me those mechanical toys, like a dog that could bark and pee and sort of walk, but obviously it hadn't been the same.

Pets were a liability. She wanted to be able to get up and move straight away. We always had our bag packed as well, just in case we had to go on the run. It had only happened once. My mother usually got her way. She was very good at manipulation.

I wouldn't have to visit Reginald today, which made me a bit sad because I realised I liked visiting him. And shirtless Dan's presence helped.

It was nearing five when I came home and I immediately went up to take a shower. I was starting to feel less exhausted by the end of my cleaning sessions, so I guess I was getting used to it. There was also a nice rhythm to my days. Clean, pub, gossip. It really did feel like a community here.

I changed into jeans and a purple blouse and went downstairs. As soon as I entered the pub, I realised how quiet it was. There were more people than usual, but they all looked like they had just witnessed someone beat a puppy.

I went to our 'usual' table where Joe and Pavani were sitting with a cold beverage in front of them. Untouched. They were staring at the table.

"Hi, guys," I said in a cheerful tone.

They both looked up. "Hey, Clara," Pavani said and exchanged a glance with Joe.

Joe had taken out his fake teeth but his cape was still draped around him as always. "I'm guessing you haven't heard?" He phrased it as a question.

"Heard what?" I glanced between him and Pavani.

"Harriet is dead," Joe said.

I felt the colour drain from my face. "What? Are you serious?"

Joe nodded with a somber expression. "Unfortunately, it is. Ignacius is with her loved ones and Ian and Marilyn are at the crime scene."

Wow, crime scene. So she really was murdered.

"Where? Where was she found?"

"In the small lake in the woods," Pavani replied. "It's between some of the Georgian estates and the village. It's relatively close to Nathan's."

"Really?" I asked.

"She was found in her car," Joe added.

"In her car?" There was so much information I had to process, I found it hard to keep up.

The door to the pub opened and Pearl strode in. She was wearing large sunglasses and a nice outfit. A little overdressed but clearly she wanted to get hired. It probably meant she didn't know about Harriet being found.

All eyes turned to her. I don't think she noticed the atmosphere and why they were all staring at her. She strode up to the bar, but I slipped out of the booth and dashed over to her. I grabbed her arm.

"Oh, hey, Clara," she started, but I interrupted her.

"Follow me." I nudged her towards the double doors to the private area. I exhaled and paused at the bottom of the stairs to my flat.

"What's going on?" she asked. She took off her sunglasses.

"You better come upstairs with me. I'll tell you."

Upstairs I made her a cup of tea and sat her down on my sofa. "I literally just heard it myself, but it seems that Harriet's body was found today."

Pearl's eyes widened for a second. "Are you serious? No, no, that can't be."

"I'm afraid so."

"But it's a prank. It has always been a prank. She just wants to get Nathan's attention. She's not dead."

"She is. She—well, I don't know how she died, but she was found in her car in the lake near your place."

She gaped at me. "We don't have a lake near our—wait, you mean that small lake in the woods? That's where she—" her voice trailed off. "I suppose that is kind of close to our place, but it's not like other places aren't close to it as well. Look, how do you know she didn't kill herself?"

"I don't. I just know she's dead and the police are looking into it. But yeah, I don't think it's a good idea to stay in the pub right now."

She jumped to her feet, spilling her tea over her hands. "I—ouch—I did not kill that woman."

"Here, let me help." I took the cup from her and led her to the kitchen so she could hold her hand under cold water.

"I'm fine," she muttered. Then she sighed heavily and dried her hands. "I don't understand any of this, Clara, I really don't. I just fell in love with Nathan and wanted to be with him. Ever since then I've faced so much judgment. I know I don't deserve Nathan, but I just want to be with him."

"You're right. You don't deserve Nathan, you deserve so much better," I said before I could stop myself.

She blinked at me.

This was not smart. "I'm sorry, I shouldn't have said that. I was out of line and it's not for me to add to the judgment."

Her features softened, to my surprise. "I know you mean well and you are very kind, but this is my business."

"Absolutely." I nodded.

"Thanks for the tea. I should go home."

"Yes, alright." I followed her to the door.

"I think you should take tomorrow off. You know, considering." She nodded at me and then walked down the stairs.

I wasn't sure if she meant our conversation or the fact that Harriet had died, but I assumed the latter. It was too bad, I was curious to learn how Nathan would handle this news.

At least it gave me the time to figure out who he owed his debt to. But first things first, I needed to know more about what happened to Harriet. I went downstairs again. I was pretty sure Pearl had left through the side entrance and inside the pub things had gotten a bit more lively. More people had come in, probably for the scoop, so people were talking now.

It also meant that Pavani had started to pitch in and I decided to do the same thing. I grabbed an apron and started helping out Agnes behind the bar. It also allowed me to catch up on the latest gossip.

According to various patrons, Harriet was apparently strangled and dumped inside the boot of her own car, which was then pushed into the lake.

That image was now stuck in my head forever. Poor Harriet.

Chapter Sixteen
From Missing to Murder

I WAS STARVING, AND it wasn't until my stomach rumbled that Agnes told me to sit down. It had been so hectic that I hadn't even noticed Marilyn arrive. She was at our usual table. I checked my watch. It was a little over eight o'clock. No wonder I was starving.

Most people had left after dinner, but new people had started arriving for a drink. At least drinks were easier to handle than food. Pavani and Agnes seemed to have things under control for now and I could always pitch in again after my food.

It struck me that I really wanted to help out Agnes. She was a very likable person. I hoped she would find help soon. It probably wasn't going to be Pearl, considering what had happened to Harriet. Gossip had already spread, and I'm sure there were plenty of people who had their eyes on Nathan or Pearl.

Marilyn would know more in any case. She was talking animatedly with Joe. I slipped into the booth next to Marilyn.

"—and the car was pushed from a small hill so it went right into the deeper end of the lake. It would have required only a little shove."

"Hi, guys," I said.

"We were just discussing Harriet's murder," Marilyn said by ways of greeting. "I wish it would quiet down so the others could join."

"Err, why? Isn't Ian going to investigate? What can we do?" They weren't seriously going to try to solve a murder, were they? Even if Marilyn was with the police, they were the neighbourhood watch.

"Are you kidding?" Joe asked. "This is a murder. We have to help any way we can. Whoever did this lives in this village. We need to keep our ears and eyes open and help in any way."

Marilyn nodded. "Exactly. Our job as the neighbourhood watch is to keep the neighbourhood safe."

I pursed my lips. They were bored. That had to be it. They were immensely bored. Even so, I had to stay on their good side. I needed their trust.

"You're right. We should do our best to help the professionals who know exactly what they're doing." Okay, I couldn't keep the sarcasm out of my voice.

"Yes, very good," Marilyn said, somehow oblivious to it.

Joe had noticed, though, and was chuckling.

Throughout the pub was the pleasant buzz of conversation, but the moment the door opened and Ian walked in, it quieted down. It wasn't as if everyone became completely silent, but the diminished volume was noticeable.

He walked straight to the bar, ordered a beer, and then joined our table. He sat down opposite me, next to Joe. "Hey," he said, then took a swig of lager.

Joe patted him on the back. "Are you alright, son? You must have had a rough day."

"Murder is never easy," I said.

Ian glanced at me as he wiped his lips with his thumb. "No, it's not. I suppose the whole village knows already."

"Yes, they do," I said. "There's a lot of gossip, though I'm not sure how much is accurate."

"I'm pretty sure the gossip is accurate," Ian said.

"So she was strangled?" I asked.

Ian nodded.

"And put in the boot of her own car?" I swallowed. My throat felt dry.

He nodded again.

Somehow I felt even more tired. "How awful."

"It is," Joe said. "She was a young lass. Such a horrible thing. Which is why it's even more important that we find out who did it."

Ian looked up at him. "Why? Did you hear anything?"

"No, but I'm sure we can find things out. We are excellent sleuths. Right, Mare?"

Marilyn nodded.

I raised an eyebrow at Ian.

"What?" he asked. "I can use all the help I can get. In case you haven't noticed, this is a small village. It has two detectives and the other one has been sick for over three years."

"I can't imagine there are a lot of murders here," I said.

"There are some, not a lot. Usually I get called to go over to other villages or assist detectives in nearby towns."

"Does that mean you're solving this on your own?" I could only imagine the pressure.

He nodded. "Yep. I phoned for assistance, but the closest town has got several big cases and they're understaffed."

"Did you speak to Dan about Harriet?" I asked.

"I did, actually. It was before her body was found. He said they just gossiped about the rich people they worked for and that was about it. He wasn't able to say anything useful on the boyfriend or anything else related to Harriet."

"That's unfortunate."

Agnes showed up at my table with a lovely vegetarian lasagna. She shoved it under my nose and despite the grim topic, I immediately went for it. I was too hungry.

"Ian, I'm so glad you're here. Are you okay?" She hugged him and then gave him a kiss on his head.

He smiled for the first time since coming in. "Yeah, I'm just really hungry."

"Say no more. I'll get you something nice. We'll talk once it quiets down." She dashed off in the direction of the kitchen.

"Calm down, you're nearly inhaling that lasagna." Joe chuckled.

I swallowed my bite before responding. "It's too delicious."

"She does make a mean lasagna," Ian said.

"She makes a mean anything." Joe's eyes twinkled. "Any dish she puts her mind to turns out wonderful. I'm telling you, she could easily be one of those celebrity chefs."

And just like that, the mood had changed. We were all smiling as Joe went on to describe his favourite dishes—he had a whole list—and added anecdotes of times she had cheered up patrons. He even claimed her fish pie had saved a fighting couple's relationship.

"Her husband easily gained weight as soon as they got married," Joe said.

This was the first time anyone mentioned Agnes's husband. I only knew from her that she wasn't blessed with kids, but that's all. My interest was immediately piqued.

"What was he like?" I asked.

"Oh, he was lovely. They doted on each other," Joe said. "They both grew up in this village and never liked each other as kids. But when they got older, things changed and they fell in love. It was very cute."

I smiled at the image of a young Agnes in love. "Did he work here as well?"

"He did. It was his idea to run the pub. Agnes did all the cooking and he did the rest. They were a good team. They poured all their love into this pub."

I wonder what other things Joe knew. He had clearly lived here a long time. "How did she end up taking care of Betty?"

"Ah, yes. Betty. She just wandered into their back garden one day and never left," Joe said.

"Really? Even though she eats purple bras?" I shook my head.

"I think that was what Agnes found endearing." Joe laughed.

It didn't surprise me, to be honest. And Betty wasn't so bad. Oh, dear. What was happening? Did I even find the sheep charming? This village was affecting me.

I finished the delicious lasagna and it wasn't until Ian had received and finished his fish and chips that we discussed the gruesome topic of murder.

By then, the pub had quieted down, even though I was convinced that some people had stuck around in the hopes of getting some more gossip out of Ian. The tables around us had stayed occupied for a while.

But now things were settling down and there were mostly a few middle-aged men at the bar, sipping on their lager. Pavani had joined us as soon as it had stopped being busy, just when Ignacius hurried in.

"I'm not too late, am I?" he asked as he sat down next to Ian, who was now sandwiched between him and Joe.

"No, we haven't discussed anything yet," Marilyn answered as she poured Pavani some Earl Grey. Even though she had been helping out Agnes for a few hours, she didn't look flustered at all. Her sweet perfume drifted my way. I hoped I would be like her when I reached eighty.

"Good." He glanced back at the bar but Agnes had already spotted him and signalled she'd get him a drink.

"How did it go?" Marilyn asked Ignacius.

"It was difficult. Harriet's mother was very upset." He winced as if he felt pain at the mere memory.

"You were there when—when Ian broke the news?" I asked.

"Yes," Ignacius said. "I wanted to offer my support in any way that I could. She's divorced, apparently, so I'm glad I went. She had nobody else to lean on."

I nodded. "That was very good of you."

"It's my job to take care of my villagers. I may not know all their names, and sometimes not even their faces—I am quite bad at that—but I do want to be there for them when they need me."

And this was probably why I'd instantly liked him. He was simply a good person.

Pavani patted his hand and he smiled at her.

I was glad I had broken away from working with my mother all those years ago. Though I couldn't really feel guilty about this con. I had dusted off all my skills for a good reason. And even if I had to leave and not see these people again, I was glad to have met them.

I glanced at Ian, who met my gaze. He gave me a smile, which I returned.

Agnes showed up with a pint for Ignacius. "How are you?" she patted him on the back.

"Fine, fine," he muttered before he put the glass to his lips and downed the entire beer in a few gulps.

The whole table gaped at him.

"What?" he asked as he wiped the foam off his lips. "I've had a long day."

"Alright." She patted his back again. "Now that we're all here and things are a lot more quiet, can we discuss what we all know?"

Joe pulled out a notebook and pen from who knows where. Perhaps his cape was magical. Everyone turned their gazes to Ian.

He cleared his throat. "Harriet was found strangled in the boot of her car, which was pushed into the lake. She had cuts on her forearms. In the boot was also her phone, but no handbag. We found her due to an anonymous tip. We don't know who called it in, but the voice indicated it was an older person, so for now we're assuming it wasn't the killer."

"Who did you talk to so far?" Agnes asked.

"I informed her mother and phoned her dad. I also talked to the boyfriend, obviously. Her parents didn't know of any potential enemies she could have had, but didn't know the boyfriend very well. He seemed upset when I told him, but he couldn't give me any useful information. I also spoke to Nathan Weatherby."

"How did he respond?" I asked.

"He became white as a sheet. He did seem visibly upset, and I doubt he's a good actor, but you never know," Ian said.

"Perhaps he was shocked that she was found so soon," Agnes said.

"Possible." Ian nodded. "He also had a black eye and claimed he walked into a door."

"What?" Agnes said.

"Oh, I actually know what that's about," I said. "I meant to tell you."

All eyes were on me this time as I told them what I'd overheard. I had intended to only tell Ian about it since Pearl didn't want anyone to know, but that was before I knew Harriet was dead.

"Underground poker games, huh?" Ian said, as I saw the cogs in his head turning. "I can't think of anyone who would do that here. I'll have to talk to him again."

"Did you talk to him about their relationship?" I was curious to know if he would deny it. He seemed to possess enough self-preservation not to lie to a detective.

"Yeah. He admitted to having a small fling. He downplayed it and said they both knew it wasn't going anywhere."

"Shallow prick," Joe said.

"We already knew he was," Agnes added with a scoff.

"Do you really think Nathan or Pearl are involved?" I asked.

Ian shrugged, but his shoulders were too tense to make it look casual. "I'm keeping an open mind."

"There was that blood in the bathroom," Ignacius said.

"And Nathan was having an affair with Harriet," Marilyn added.

I tapped my chin. "And the car was found relatively close to their place. But why wouldn't he have cleaned up the blood? Also, if she was strangled, why was there blood?"

Everyone was quiet for a moment as we all contemplated this.

Ian broke the silence. "There was something odd."

He had us hanging from his lips. His very soft-looking lips. *Focus.*

"On her computer we found out she had searched for poisonous plants. Lethal plants." He glanced around the table, letting the words sink in. "I don't know why, but it's the reason my boss thought it was a suicide, combined with that letter. But the letter didn't sit right with me and now it turns out she was strangled."

"Poisonous plants," I said more to myself than anyone else. That was odd. "Could her boyfriend have looked those up?"

"I asked him and he said he didn't know anything about it. Of course, he could be lying, but why?"

More questions than answers. It seemed a real-life murder case was quite tricky indeed.

Chapter Seventeen
A New Client

IT WAS FRIDAY NIGHT so I could sleep in tomorrow, which was good because we ended up chatting until midnight. Not that we had uncovered some sort of plan of action or any new clues. There was little we could do except keep our eyes and ears open, and to be honest, I didn't really want to get involved. I had my main mission to think of.

I yawned as I entered my bedroom and was about to change into my pyjamas when I heard something clattering in the alley. I opened the doors to the French balcony and already spotted Ian hanging over his, staring down.

I followed his gaze to the creature that scuttled about in the darkness. A fluffy tale gave away that it was a fox and not a cat.

"Is this the infamous Lola?" I asked.

The fox's ears twitched and she looked up at me.

"Hi, Lola." I waved.

"It is. Agnes sometimes leaves a plate with scraps for her."

"Aha, so it's really Agnes's fault she shows up."

Ian looked up at me. "You say that as if it's a bad thing. Don't you like foxes?"

"I guess," I said. "I prefer a dog."

"Really? Why don't you have one, then?"

"I have a job. It's just not handy." I tucked a strand of my auburn hair behind my ear. There was a gentle wind. "What about you? No pets?"

"No. After my divorce I turned into a bit of a workaholic."

I nodded. "I understand that. It must have been quite the change, going from married to single."

"It was."

"But hey, at least Agnes can go crazy and set you up left and right."

He laughed. "Even though she enjoys playing matchmaker, she's only tried setting me up with one person."

We both knew who that person was.

"I see," I said, not sure what else to say. We had never really discussed going out again. I yawned, feeling exhausted from this entire day. "I should go to sleep. I'll see you."

"Hey," Ian said, straightening. "Do me a favour and be careful, especially around Weatherby. Just in case."

We stared at each for a moment.

"Okay, I promise." I went back inside, closed the doors and pulled the curtains over them. I sighed. Why did he have to be so nice?

My phone chimed. Before picking it up, I changed into my pyjamas, brushed my teeth and removed my makeup. I then hopped into bed and checked my phone.

An email from my mother.

HONEY,

How are you? I hope you are taking good care of yourself. It was great seeing you last time, thanks for coming. It would be nice to see you again soon. I know you said you'd help me get the money for the experimental treatment, but I don't want you to feel pressured. All things considered, I'm doing quite well. Although I did have a dizzy spell yesterday, but Rod is taking good care of me.

Lots of love,
Your favourite mother

I FELT MY STRESS LEVELS increase as I read it. Things had been bad between us ever since I decided to quit the 'family business' and I hadn't seen my mother in forever. She and Rod were still working together, and whenever I did talk to my mum she made sure to guilt trip me.

The thing is, I knew I was good at conning, just like my mum was, but I just didn't want to do it. The older I became, the richer the targets, but just because they could spare the money, didn't mean we should take it from them.

Then I got the message that she was sick and she wanted me to visit. She gave me her mother's ring and it had felt like goodbye even though the doctor had given her about a year to two years.

That's when I had decided on one more con. If I could get my mum that treatment, perhaps there was a chance I wouldn't lose her.

No, she hadn't been a good mother, but she was kind of all I had. Right?

I emailed her back, telling her not to worry and that I would help her out. At least she had Rod to look after her. It would have to do until I could go back and stay by her side. I didn't know how our relationship would be afterwards, and if she'd continue to con, but I wanted to be there for her. I just had to do this first.

THE NEXT MORNING I slept in until nine o'clock and made myself a nice breakfast consisting of buttered toast and two eggs, sunny side up. It was nowhere near as good as anything Agnes could make, but it didn't matter. I still felt like I was spoiling myself.

I risked a glance into my neighbouring flat and caught sight of a shirtless Ian. *Oh, boy.* I couldn't see that well into his flat, but enough to notice his fine abs. I didn't want to stare so I looked away. I could hardly stand there and gape at him. At least he hadn't seen me look.

I grabbed my tea and plate and moved in front of the TV and settled on an episode of *Father Brown*. It seemed fitting with everything that was going on.

After breakfast, I took a shower and got dressed. Despite the fact that I didn't want to get involved in the murder, it had been on my mind most of the morning. I had even dreamt about being chased by the killer. I couldn't help but wonder if I could use my particular skill set to apprehend the person who did this to Harriet, but I wasn't sure how. I had never solved a murder, nor did I know where to begin. Ian was the expert.

Still, I finally understood the neighbourhood watch better. The idea of this monster getting away with it was very unsettling.

I grabbed the business card Pearl had given me of her friend. I was going to pay her a visit in person and check if she still wanted to hire me. Pearl had made it sound like it was a done deal, but I wanted to see for myself.

After that I'd explore the village. I still had to do that and I was looking forward to a casual stroll. It would be interesting to see what these villagers did on a Saturday.

DARLA LIVED IN A LARGE detached property. It wasn't as impressive as Nathan's Georgian estate, but it was definitely fancy and expensive. The two BMWs also proved wealthy people lived here. It wouldn't surprise me if they had built this house themselves. It was very modern.

I rang the doorbell as I studied their front garden. There were zero plants. A lot of hedges for privacy, but that was it. I wondered what these people did for a living.

A heavily perfumed woman opened the door. She had a stout figure but was most likely wearing spandex. Or perhaps it was liposuction? Judging by the tight expression on her face she was also no stranger to Botox. She had to be in her fifties, but was trying very hard to look thirty.

She smiled at me. "Yes?"

"Hi," I said in my most cheerful tone. "I'm Clara. I was told you are in need of a maid."

Her eyebrows shot up, though they didn't get very far. "How did you know that?"

"I was referred to you by Pearl."

Her nose wrinkled, but it was so brief I almost missed it. Okay, so she didn't like Pearl. How strange, I got the impression they were friends. *Maybe Pearl wants to get on her good side, or perhaps rumours about Harriet have affected her opinion on Nathan and Pearl?*

"Was she wrong? Do you not need a maid?" I asked, pretending I had misinterpreted her reaction.

"No, no. We spoke about you a short while ago. It had just slipped my mind. Why don't you come in?" She stepped aside.

"Thank you." The hallway was spacious and decorated tastefully with several floral paintings. The floor looked like it was made of marble and there was a table with a colourful vase with flowers in the middle.

"Follow me into the reception room," she said and preceded me into the next area. Her heels were thin and high. *Impressive.*

There was a modern fireplace in the back of the room and two sofas placed opposite each other. They looked expensive. Everything so far looked expensive. I glanced down at the Persian rug under my feet. She also had on a diamond necklace and several white gold rings.

It was an old habit to pay attention to any potentially expensive items. It's how my mother picked her targets. It always started somewhere in public, a seemingly innocent encounter. She'd always do or say something to ramp up their empathy but at the same time make herself valuable to them. They had to have the idea that they needed her.

Right now, Darla needed me. It was a small village and I was certain that most of the rich clients I had encountered so far knew my target. But if not, they could at least lead me to someone who did. I knew he lived on the outskirts of this village, but not exactly where and I didn't want to come outright and ask. Not to mention, not knowing his surname didn't help. Subtlety was the name of the game.

"You have a lovely home," I said. There was nothing wrong with a bit of flattery. It had the tendency to lower people's guards. It didn't even matter if it was true or not; people heard what they wanted to hear.

"Thank you, I know. My husband knows people. They helped build this place from the ground up. Took only six months. We have it exactly as we like it," she said. "Do you want tea?"

"That would be lovely." I smiled at her.

She sighed as if it was a chore, but got up and left the room.

I exhaled. I didn't know why I was feeling nervous, but I was. Perhaps because I felt the pressure. I wanted to hurry up and find him. Even if I did, I would still have to put things in motion and gain his trust, but even so. It was my mum's email. It had unsettled me.

She returned with two delicate cups of tea. I refrained from making a face. Sure, they were very ornate, but they were hardly big enough for ten drops of tea. I preferred a big mug any day of the week.

Luckily, she had brought out biscuits. I took one and nibbled on it so that my tea could cool off.

"So, you're new to the village, then?" Darla asked.

"Yes, I am. I just moved here. I live above the pub."

She wrinkled her nose again. "The one with the sheep?"

I wasn't sure if she was referring to the name of the pub or Betty. "Yes, that's the one."

"Interesting," she said in a tone that indicated it was not.

After I had finished my biscuit, I tried the tea. It was actually really nice. "So, how often would you require my service?" I asked her.

She nodded. "Twice a week only. It's just for the bathroom and bedrooms. The rest I can manage on my own. I don't mind cleaning."

"Neither do I," I said with a chuckle.

"I should hope not or otherwise you're in the wrong business."

"It was a joke," I mumbled and took another sip of my tea.

"How long have you been cleaning?"

"Several years now," I said. The lie easily rolled off my tongue. My latest jobs were as a bartender and shop assistant. Both were quite boring, though working at a bar could be fun sometimes.

"Do you need a reference?" I maintained a smile. If she said yes, I could arrange that. I had some old friends who would help me out and lie for me. Well, they were good acquaintances, more like.

"No, that won't be necessary. I suppose I'll hire you but it will be on a trial basis first. I want to see how you do before I permanently hire you. I hope that's okay."

"Sure. Not a problem at all." Before she would send me off, I wanted to poke around the subject of Nathan and Pearl a bit more. "If you want to know more about what I'm like as a maid, I don't mind you asking Pearl or Nathan about me. I'm sure they'll tell you exactly what they think of my service."

This time she pursed her lips. "I'd rather not."

"Why not?"

"Didn't you hear about that maid of theirs that got murdered? Are you not uncomfortable still working for them?"

My jaw tensed. "I did hear about Harriet's death, yes. It is very tragic, but since we don't know who committed the crime, it seems quite awful to just assume who the killer is." I didn't like Nathan, but I wasn't sure if he was a murderer and the only crime Pearl seemed to have committed was saying yes to Nathan. Of course, it could be that one of them killed Harriet, but even so, without evidence it seemed wrong to judge either of them.

"Not just anyone. Nathan Weatherby has always been a despicable human being and though I liked Pearl, I don't think she is the best judge of character."

So it's Nathan she suspects and not Pearl. "Do you really think Nathan killed Harriet? Do you think I could be in danger?" I asked, hoping she'd explain to me why she thought he was so awful. I mean, it was pretty obvious, I suppose, but I sensed a story.

"I hope not, but I wouldn't put it past him. He's a cheating poker addict."

Aha.

"Came to borrow my husband's money and he never saw a penny of it. Scoundrel," she cursed under her breath.

"I did hear that he had a poker problem. And that he was involved with that guy Lou." It was the only name I could think of.

She tossed back her head and laughed. "You mean Big Jimmy? He's some sort of pathetic gangster that has Nathan weeing himself in fear. He tried to put the screws on my husband once when he tried to help Nathan. Learned his lesson. He's on his own and you should probably stay clear of either of them."

"Duly noted," I said, beyond ecstatic that I had a name.

"Anyways, you can start next week."

"Perfect." We discussed the final details and I gave her my number before she let me out. I was finally getting somewhere. Both with my mission and with the murder.

Chapter Eighteen
Exploring Greystone

I parked my car by the pub, but didn't go back up to my flat. It was time to take a stroll around Greystone. I also wanted to pay a visit to the bookshop next to the pub, but I figured I'd end my walk there.

I turned left and ventured down the cobbled street. There were several shops: one that sold expensive-looking soaps and bath stuff, one that sold anything related to outdoor activities, and even a cupcake place. I was tempted to buy a cupcake, but decided I wanted to keep on moving.

When I reached the end of the street, I overlooked a small park. The church was on the other side and to the right was the post office. To the left was a beautiful thatched property that Ignacius was just leaving.

He seemed to have had a rough day yesterday so I decided to catch up to him on his way to the church.

"Ignacius," I said, hardly out of breath. "Hey."

He turned around. "Clara, how nice to see you on this beautiful Saturday."

I narrowed my eyes at him. "You're very cheerful."

"Of course. Why wouldn't I be? Isn't it a lovely day?"

The sun was indeed shining and it was warm enough for me to have left my leather jacket at home. "I suppose it is."

I started walking next to him, my hands in my pocket. "So, you're alright then?"

"Yes. Why wouldn't I be?"

"Yesterday was really tough, wasn't it?" How could he seem utterly unaffected? Yesterday he was definitely not that cheerful. Had he really gotten over it that quickly?

"Of course, but it benefits nobody if I go around sulking. It's a new day and there are new opportunities." We reached the church and stopped for a moment as we both regarded the building. It wasn't a large church but that was because it wasn't a large village.

"Are you going to say God works in mysterious ways?" I asked.

"If there are mysterious forces at work, I'd like to think they have their reasons, but then again, it could all just be chance. Perhaps Harriet was at the wrong place and time and suffered the worst luck of all."

I pursed my lips as I regarded him. "Why did you become a vicar?"

He smiled, but it was a rather sad smile. "Because I believed in something bigger than myself."

"Past tense?"

"Indeed." He looked in the direction of the park and sighed. "You see, just as I had started working as a vicar, I fell head over heels in love. I don't want to be too dramatic, but it really felt like she was my soulmate. It was as if lightning had struck me."

He had my interest. Did this mean true love did exist?

"We were crazy about each other and it felt like everything I had done was in order to meet her. I know that may sound silly, but that's how it felt. Anyway, one time we were driving to a birthday party of one of her relatives and we got into a car accident." He bent down and touched his prosthetic leg. "Hence the leg. Unfortunately, I lost worse than that."

I gasped. "No. She died?"

He nodded as the corner of his lips quivered for just a second. "It was the worst time of my life. And I realised I didn't believe anymore. It's as simple as that."

This was the saddest thing I'd ever heard. "Is that why your other marriages didn't work out?"

He touched his chin. "Why do you say that?"

I shrugged. "I can imagine somewhere along the line you'd want to experience something similar to that first love, but by always comparing those relationships to the first one I can imagine it would never feel right. Besides, by losing your faith in God didn't you simultaneously lose your faith in love? At least, I think I would wonder about the point of it all. Since you can lose someone just like that."

He stared at me. "I suppose I had never thought of it that way. You're very astute."

"I could be wrong. Anyway, I'm very sorry. You both deserved your happy ending." I touched his shoulder. This man still had the strength to stay cheerful and help people even though he suffered a great deal of pain. I couldn't help but feel for him.

"Oh, dear. You are very sweet. Don't make me cry now." He reached up and squeezed my hand.

I smiled at him. "Thanks for telling me this."

"You are very welcome. Now, let's talk about something more cheerful. Tonight is the pub quiz. Are you joining? We are awfully... bad."

I laughed. "Way to sell it."

He chuckled. "I figured I wouldn't get your hopes up. We like to think we know a lot, but the pub quiz proves we don't. Still, we have a lot of fun."

"And by 'we' you mean the neighbourhood watch, right?"

He nodded. "Are you in? Say you're in."

"I'm in."

"Wonderful. I look forward to seeing you then." He gave me a kiss on the cheek and then limped off towards the church.

I sighed as I watched him go. He had good friends in this village and it's not as if he was unhappy, but I hated sad endings. I made sure I always read romance novels where the couple got together because I knew things like this happened in real life. Real life was stupid.

I continued wandering around the village, checking out the various cottages and cosy homes I walked by. Most of them had garden gnomes in their front garden and there were lots of flowers and plants to make the cottages more lively. It seemed that most people were out and about and I wasn't the only one walking through the village. I also noted that a lot of people cycled and whenever anyone passed me, they greeted me.

After I had soaked up the beauty of this village, I returned towards the pub. This time I did buy a cupcake. A vanilla velvet one with sprinkles from a woman who introduced herself as Amelia. She had black hair, blue eyes and a round figure. She stood out because of her fifties swing dress and hairstyle. I loved it since my maid outfit was in a similar style.

Despite the fact that her shop—*Amelia's*—was busy, she did ask me a few questions. I guess it was inevitable since I was the newbie and I lived close-by, but just as before I remained vague and deflected.

She told me she had started her cupcake shop five years ago and gave me the first one on the house. The first bite was divine. Her skills rivaled Agnes's but with cupcakes. I definitely would be coming here more often.

After the cupcake shop, I went into the bookshop next to the pub. I remembered the owner was Ian's landlord. His name was Harry.

The bookshop was small and dusty, but it had a certain charm. I instantly felt at home there. I knew I couldn't buy any of the books, because I'd be forced to leave them behind once I left this place, but I still enjoyed the browse.

It wasn't terribly busy and I moved forward towards the romance section. A middle-aged man was behind the counter. His hair was grey and he had a round face with red cheeks. I contemplated saying hi to him. He was also the father of Dylan—Harriet's boyfriend. Should I offer my condolences? Were they close? He had been the one to ask Ian to look into her disappearance when she hadn't come home.

There was a doorway behind the counter. Harry glanced in its direction. "How is it going, son?" he asked.

Wait, he was here?

"Fine." A young man with shaggy dark-blond hair emerged from the other room carrying a box. "Where do you want this?"

"That display over there." He pointed to a spot in the shop and I looked away. I didn't want to make it too obvious I was observing them.

"Okay," Dylan said as he went on his way.

He had no bags under his eyes, no sadness about him whatsoever, but it didn't necessarily mean something. Still, I filed away that information. I wondered why he was working in his dad's bookshop. Ian hadn't mentioned it.

I decided to approach the counter with a demure smile. "Hello, you must be Harry," I said and held out my hand with reluctance.

He shook it with a smile. His hands felt warm. "I am. And you are?"

"I'm Clara. I'm new here. I'm staying above the pub."

His smile faded. "Ah, you're the new maid."

"I am. I suppose news travels fast." I decided to play dumb and pretend I didn't know what Harry's connection to Harriet was.

"Yes, well, you must have met poor Harriet," he said.

"I did. She was lovely. I'm horrified about what happened to her."

He nodded, the corners of his mouth turned down. "She was my son's girlfriend." He nodded towards Dylan.

I glanced over my shoulder at him. He was working on a display.

"Oh, no. I'm so sorry," I said to Harry. "I had no idea. That is awful. How is your son doing?"

"He's hanging in there. Harriet was the breadwinner so I offered him to work for me, but really, I'm overstaffed. Not that it matters, mind you. It's the least of my worries. I just want him to be okay. I'm sure Ian will figure out what happened. You must know him, right?"

"Ian?" I said, managing to keep my voice steady. "Yeah, I've seen him around."

"He's a good man. He will sort this whole mess out."

"I'm sure he will. Do you mind if I go and offer my condolences to your son?" I gave him a sad smile.

"Of course, that is very kind of you. It was a pleasure meeting you." He reached out and shook my hand again.

Great.

"You too."

Dylan was very focussed as he carefully stacked a few new sci-fi books on the display table. He hadn't even noticed me approach.

"Dylan, right?" I asked and gave him the same smile I had given his father. I didn't want to appear too happy, but at the same time a smile was charming. I needed him to be charmed.

"Yeah, how do you know that?" Unlike his dad he was a bit more suspicious about how I knew his name.

"Your dad told me," I said as I pointed back to the counter. "I'm Clara. I'm new here and I worked with Harriet. She seemed lovely, and I just wanted to express my sympathy."

His face turned pale. "I appreciate that."

"How are you holding up?"

His brown eyes scanned my face. "It's rough, I'm not going to lie. I keep expecting her to show up. It's like it's not real, you know?"

I nodded. "I can understand that. Were you together long?"

"Three years," he said. "But I—I'd been planning on breaking up with her. I just didn't expect this to happen. I mean, I'm glad I didn't because that would have just been even more awful, wouldn't it? It just—well, she was working all the time. We hardly laughed together anymore."

"I'm sorry. Well, she talked about you all the time when we worked together." I wanted to see his reaction to that. He said he wanted to break up because she was working a lot, but maybe he had known about Nathan.

His eyes widened and there was something hopeful about his expression. "Really? She mentioned me?"

Was he surprised because of their deteriorating relationship or because he knew she'd been cheating?

"She did. It was clear she loved you very much."

His bottom lip started to tremble and his eyes filled with tears.

Uh-oh.

"Excuse me," he said softly and brushed past me as he hurried off.

I bit my lip. I hadn't meant to make him cry, but it had been an interesting reaction. Perhaps it was because he had heard rumours about Harriet and Nathan and doubted how much she cared for him. Or perhaps because he felt guilty about breaking up with her.

"Making men cry?" Ian's voice sounded behind me.

I turned around. "I can assure you I'm as sweet as a kitten."

"You know kittens have claws, right?"

"What are you doing here?" I crossed my arms.

"Just checking up on Dylan. Seeing how he's doing. Why? Am I not allowed to do that?"

"Not at all," I said. In fact, it was smart. "I can already tell you that he seemed surprised when I told him Harriet talked about him all the time. It could be that he's heard rumours about her and Nathan. Or maybe he knew about them beforehand. He also said he was planning on breaking up with her."

"Sleuthing, are we?"

"Well, I am in the neighbourhood watch."

He smiled at me. "Just be careful."

"Always."

"But thank you for letting me know."

"No problem," I said.

"I'll see you at the pub quiz." He flashed me one final smile and walked into the direction of the counter.

Oh, no. And here I thought it was just going to be the neighbourhood watch. Why had I said yes?

Chapter Nineteen
Gossip Girls

MY INITIAL PLAN HAD been to eat lunch in my flat, but I was too tempted by Agnes's way with food so I sat down in the pub. Agnes officially had me hooked.

I had only just sat down when a shadow fell over me.

"Can I take your order?" a female voice asked.

I looked up into Pearl's eyes. "Pearl?"

"Yeah. I followed your advice and asked for a job here."

I gaped at her in surprise. "When?"

"This morning, on the phone. Agnes hired me straight away." She beamed with pride.

I glanced around. People didn't appear to be staring. "And nobody has been..." I was trying to look for the right word.

"Prying? Or clearly gossiping about me?" she asked. "Yeah, but I can handle it. It seems their interest dies down quickly when you don't respond."

Wow. She was a lot stronger than I thought. "Good for you," I said with a smile.

"Thank you." She smiled back. "Now, what can I get you?"

"A goat's cheese sandwich, please. And a lemonade."

"You got it." She winked at me and went to pass on my order.

At least Agnes was getting the help she needed, but I also had the feeling she wanted to keep Pearl close for neighbourhood watch reasons.

I couldn't exactly blame her since I had talked to Dylan. It was busier now that it was Saturday but I hadn't spotted anyone from the neighbourhood watch. Ignacius was at the church, but I wondered what the others were doing. Was Pavani teaching yoga? I hadn't checked out her studio yet. I was actually curious about it.

And Joe. Was he skulking about in the cemetery? Or did he actually have hobbies?

Oh, no. Was I starting to care? I had to keep my eye on the ball. Especially now that I was getting closer to my goal.

Pearl brought over my plate. She looked completely at ease in her apron as she smiled at arriving or departing patrons. Even with me she was fully accommodating even though I was her maid. While she was in work mode, she completely embraced the role as waitress.

"Agnes told me you went on a date with that detective, Ian," Pearl said and got a glint in her eyes.

"Err, it wasn't really a date," I said. Great, Agnes was spreading rumours about us. It wouldn't surprise me if she was secretly planning our wedding.

"Don't be shy. Give me some details. He is quite handsome, I suppose. Did you guys kiss?"

She was actually gossiping with me. Like a friend. How interesting. Even after I broke away from my mother, I never really got attached enough to make true friends. I had too many walls around me, courtesy of mummy dearest.

What if I had approached this all wrong? By trying to push these people away I would only make myself look more suspicious. What if this was my chance to experience what it was like to be normal? Sure, it would make it more difficult to vanish without a trace once I was done, but if I had to be honest, it would be tricky no matter what. This was a lovely place with lovely people. Instead of wondering what could have been in a different life, I could actually experience it.

"No, but I did kiss him on his cheek," I replied.

Her smile widened. "Really? How did he react?"

"As I recall he scanned my face." He had also said he'd keep an eye on me, but let's not mention that.

"Oh, I love it." She clasped her hands. "I need to get back to work, but you need to tell me more later. Oh, speak of the devil." She winked at me and walked over to another table while I watched Ian enter the pub, make eye contact and then head over.

I swallowed as he sat down opposite me.

"Long time no see. Having lunch?"

"Yep," I said. Thanks to Pearl the memory of our non-date was still bouncing around in my head and it made me nervous for some reason. I was never nervous. Not even during cons.

Ian studied my face. "Are you okay?"

"Yeah, fine. Why wouldn't I be?" I managed a smile. Did it look weird? It felt weird.

He frowned and was about to say something when Pearl showed up at our table.

"Hello, Detective," she said with a charming smile. "How are you today?"

Ian stared at her for a moment, clearly as surprised as I had been. "Pearl. What are you doing here?"

She laughed. It sounded melodious. "You're supposed to be good at deductive reasoning," she said. "I'm working here. Agnes needs a hand and I need the money." She flushed at that, as if she regretted it. "I mean, I don't need it, I want it. To buy a surprise for Nathan."

She wasn't a very good liar. Her lack of eye contact gave her away.

"Anyway, what can I get you?"

"A lemonade and a chicken sandwich. Thank you."

"No problem," she said. "Enjoy your date."

"It's not a—" I started, but she was already gone.

Ian had a cheeky grin on his face.

"Agnes has been saying things," I said.

"We can't have that, can we? It will ruin my reputation."

I laughed.

His grin transformed into a broad smile. He had a mesmerising smile.

"Anyway, did Dylan give you any more information?" I took a bite out of my sandwich.

"He didn't. He seemed genuinely upset and asked me if I knew who had killed her. I had to tell him no. To make things worse, his dad kept saying I'd solve the case." He ran a hand through his hair, messing it up, though that somehow looked cute on him.

"I'm sorry. That must be a lot of pressure. Don't let it get to you. You can only do your best," I said.

His gaze softened. "I know. Thank you. I told them that."

I wondered if this murder case reminded him of his mother's case. I wondered if every murder case did. Did he feel intense pressure to solve his cases because he knew what it was like to not know as a relative?

"Sometimes bad things happen," I said. "And sometimes bad people get away with bad things. That's on them, not you."

He rested his head on his fist but didn't say anything. Why was he looking at me like that? "What? Impressed by my wisdom?"

"No, I'm impressed by your ability to make me feel better with just your words."

My throat suddenly felt dry and I had to take a sip of my lemonade. I had to change the topic. "I forgot to tell you something about Nathan," I said, eyeing the pub to make sure Pearl wasn't close.

He sat up straight. "Did he do something?"

"No, no. Well, not with me." I picked up a walnut from my plate and stuck it in my mouth. "Did you talk to Nathan about the poker and his debt?"

"Yes, actually. He was my first stop this morning." He didn't say anything else.

"And?"

"And I know who he's indebted to."

I narrowed my eyes at him. "You're not going to tell me who."

"Bingo."

"Why not?"

"Because I don't need you to know. I know how easily the neighbourhood watch can get swept up in things. Just being safe rather than sorry."

I guess I didn't need to tell him then. It also meant I had to find out where Big Jimmy held his games another way.

"So you think that this debt has anything to do with Harriet's death?" I asked.

"I doubt it, but I am keeping an open mind. Nathan was involved with her and though he claimed she had nothing to do with his poker problems, you never know."

I thought back to my mother and how she made sure she was valuable to her targets. Harriet seemed to be very eager to be by Nathan's side and live a richer life. She would have wanted to get in his good graces. "What if she wanted to help him with his debt? What if she promised to take care of it or something like that?" If he had gone to friends to ask for money, he would have been desperate enough to accept the help of his mistress.

"How would she have helped him?" Ian asked.

"I don't know."

"If she did, I will find out." But he didn't look convinced. I could understand why. I hadn't met Big Jimmy, but men like that didn't talk to the police. Not even if they had committed a crime in front of a police officer. Even if Ian threatened him with obstruction of justice, he wouldn't care. Talking to the police would be bad for business, and it's not like Ian had anything on him.

I could still execute my plan.

Pearl showed up with Ian's order. "Enjoy," she said in a high voice and then winked at me.

Ian didn't seem phased by it and dug into his sandwich. I had nearly finished mine and enjoyed watching him eat.

"So, are you good at pub quizzes?" I asked when we were both done and Pearl had taken away our plates. "Because Ignacius said you were all bad."

"I've rarely joined. But it is always fun."

I wondered what made him join this time, but I was afraid to ask. "Okay." I glanced at my phone to check the time.

"What's wrong? Places to be?" Ian's lips curved into a grin.

Pearl would be here for a while, which meant that Nathan was home alone. It was the perfect time to find out where this Big Jimmy could be found. However, if I asked him directly, he'd know I was looking into the murder. If he really was the killer that would be bad. Also, I had promised Pearl I wouldn't tell anyone I knew. Granted, I'd already broken my promise, but I didn't want to land her in hot water with Nathan, especially if he was the killer.

The only other person I knew who could help me was Darla's husband.

"Actually, I do. I'll see you back here for dinner." I got up from the booth.

"Is that a date?" he asked.

I froze. Gossiping with Pearl was one thing, but letting my guard down around Ian was very dangerous. I didn't need to break my heart, nor his.

"Not at all," I said. Then turned and left through the double doors. They had just shut behind me when I toppled over and smacked onto the floor with a thud.

"I deserved that," I groaned and opened my eyes.

Betty was sniffing my forehead. "Baaaaa," she said.

"Baaa back." I pushed myself up, groaning. "You know you're hitting close to thirty when you can't get up without making noises," I said out loud.

Betty started nibbling on my blue pullover. "No, no. Naughty Betty." I grabbed her by her collar and directed her through the private kitchen and back into the garden where she stood staring at me. She looked disappointed to be in the garden again.

Right. Back to my second mission. Time to find out where this Big Jimmy held his poker matches.

Chapter Twenty
The Pub Quiz

I WENT UPSTAIRS AND Googled Darla West's name. A local newspaper article popped up about her and her husband. She apparently did a lot of charity work and he ran a modeling agency. In other words, his website and contact details were easy to find.

I dialed the number and the phone only rang once before he answered.

"West," he said in a gruff voice.

"Yeah, hello, this is Veronica. Nathan Weatherby gave me your contact info. I'm a friend of his and I need to know where Big Jimmy has his poker matches."

It was silent for a few moments.

"Why not ask him then?"

"Haven't you heard about his maid's murder? They're watching his every move, even his phone. He doesn't want them to know about his debt and asked me to help out. They beat him up, you know? He's pretty spooked."

Silence again.

"Look, all you have to do is tell me where the matches are being held."

West sighed. "There's a nightclub in South Bedring called Hot Stuff. Just be careful, love. Like you already know, they hurt people. And Nathan only looks out for himself."

"Thanks. Bye." I hung up. This was good. South Bedring was the nearest city so the drive wouldn't be too long. I googled the nightclub. It was open until 2 o'clock. The pub quiz would hardly last long. If I made sure I left at eleven, I'd be there before midnight. Enough time to do my thing.

I rubbed my hands and found myself smiling at the prospect. This time I wouldn't have to feel guilty because it was for a good cause.

THE WHOLE GANG WAS present at the pub during dinner time, except for Ian. Agnes was working the bar with Pearl. All the women were on one side of the booth, and the men on the other side. This time Ignacius was across from me and Joe was by the window.

"Ooh, just in time," Pavani said as she nudged me. "We are about to order."

"Good. I'm hungry."

"What have you been up to today?" Joe asked me. "Are you free on weekends?"

"I am. I just took a stroll around the village. Nothing special." I didn't want to tell them about Big Jimmy in case they wanted to get involved, and also I didn't want to get their hopes up. There was a very distinct possibility that Nathan's debt had nothing to do with Harriet's murder.

"Did you see Mr Willoughby's ass?" Pavani asked, a cheeky grin on her face.

"Excuse you?" I said.

Everybody sniggered at my response.

Marilyn leaned forward so she could see past Pavani. "Mr Willoughby has a donkey in his front garden. It's a large fenced garden, but it always attracts a lot of attention from non-villagers or newbies such as yourself. Nobody expects there to be a donkey."

"I see. Where does he live?"

"Behind the church, close to the woods," Ignacius said. "His donkey is quite old and rarely moves from its spot, but he's also very soft and a lot of the kids stop by to pet him."

"Does he have a name?" I asked.

"You know what? I actually don't know," Ignacius said.

"No, he doesn't," Joe replied. "We just call him Mr Willoughby's ass."

I laughed. "As long as this ass isn't as hungry as Betty, I think I'm okay with it."

"Can I get you guys anything?" Pearl showed up at our table. She didn't have a hair out of place and didn't look flustered at all. She was clearly a pro at this.

I ordered shepherd's pie and a red wine. We all chatted amicably until our dinners came and then we were distracted by the deliciousness of the food. The meat was perfectly seasoned and the mashed potatoes were well browned. All the flavours merged wonderfully in my mouth. The wine was sweet and complemented the meal.

"Do you like our village so far?" Pavani asked as she pushed her empty plate away. She also had that content look on her face after eating one of Agnes's meals.

"I do. It is a charming place," I said. "Have you lived here long?"

"Since my fifties. I felt quite lonely after I got divorced and my only child moved to Australia. I was teaching yoga already and one of my clients recommended a holiday to Greystone. I decided to go for it, especially since it's so beautiful here and I love hiking as well. Anyway, I fell in love with the people and this place."

"I had no idea you had a child who moved to Australia."

"A daughter, yes. She decided to study marine biology and well, she loves her job there. To top it all off, she met an Australian bloke there and now she's married with kids."

"And do you see your grandchildren often?"

She sighed and a sadness fell over her. "No. I'd love to see them more, but I am anchored to this place. I wouldn't want to move to Australia at all, and I know they don't want to move. So it is what it is. At least we have the technology to keep in touch. I'm thankful for that."

I nodded and couldn't help but wonder what it would have been like to have someone like Pavani as my mother. Or Agnes. My life would have been so different.

Oh, well. No point dwelling on what could have been.

It was almost eight o'clock, which was when the pub quiz would start. It was also when Ian showed up and joined our table. He sat down next to Ignacius and opposite me.

"Are you guys ready for the pub quiz?" he asked.

"Oh, we are. It's going to be fun," Ignacius said. He looked at me. "You are in for a treat."

I smiled. "I am?"

Joe leaned forward with an excited glint in his eyes. "This pub quiz is a special edition."

I raised an eyebrow. "It is? In what way?"

"Normally it's about all sorts of trivia, right?" he said. "But this time it's trivia about this village. Only the locals are participating and right now that's you, too." He winked at me.

They considered me a local, huh? "That's very sweet, but it also means I'll be a rubbish participant. I know very little about Greystone."

"Exactly." Ian grinned. "This way you get to learn lots about all of us."

Something in my chest tightened. Had they done this just for me?

"I see." I really didn't know what else to say.

"You've been so helpful with the neighbourhood watch and despite everything that has happened, you're a real trooper," Joe said.

Okay, that answered that question.

"That's very sweet of you, guys. But you didn't have to do that."

"Are you joking?" Marilyn said. "You found the blood in the bathroom and still wanted to help out. Not everyone would have done that."

I pressed my lips together. Would I have joined the neighbourhood watch if I hadn't wanted to get in their good books or get information? Probably not. Then again, I hardly would have come here otherwise. My previous home was a small flat near my latest job as a travel agent. It was actually the first job I genuinely liked. It was also the first office job I had managed to secure for myself. I had been very proud of myself. Still, it would have been a very long time until I would be able to af-ford living in a village like this. It had been luck or maybe even fate that Agnes had a place I could rent relatively cheap.

"She's right," Ian added. "You barely knew Harriet and yet you're doing your best to brainstorm and help out."

"Anyone would do the same."

"No, not everyone would." He held my gaze. "You're quite brave."

I had never considered myself that, but I suppose I was braver than the average person. My mum always taught me that fear was a normal part of life. It wasn't anything to shy away from and definitely wasn't a reason not to do something.

"Thanks," I said with a polite smile. These compliments were unnerving. I just wasn't used to them. "So, do we need pen and paper or anything? When are we starting?"

Ian smiled to himself, probably realising I was changing the topic.

"Agnes will start in a minute and then she'll hand out our answer sheets and a bunch of pens," Ignacius said. "It will be handy to have one person do the writing. Usually we take turns, but maybe it's nice if you do the writing this time."

"So Agnes is not participating?" I asked.

Pavani shook her head. "Oh, no. She's created all the ques-tions, so it would be very unfair. She's always the host. And she's also the one that hands out the prize."

I licked my lips. "There's a prize? Is it food?"

They all chuckled.

"I wish," Joe muttered. "But no, it's always a trophy with some sweets or something. It's a tiny trophy so don't get your hopes up."

"I don't expect to win anyway. If all the participants are locals it's going to be tricky to win."

"True," Pavani said. "But it wouldn't be a challenge otherwise. And challenges are fun."

Depends on the challenge.

The pub got crowded very soon and people sat together in groups, talking and laughing until Agnes grabbed a microphone and took place in front of the bar.

"Hello, lovely people. It's Saturday and therefore time for the pub quiz!" Despite the fact that she'd been working all day, she looked lovely. Her cheeks were rosy and she grinned excitedly.

Everybody clapped and a few guys whistled and cheered. I smiled at their enthusiasm.

"We have special questions planned and that is why only locals could sign up for today's quiz."

A few people cheered again.

"I'll be handing out your answer sheets and then we can start. We have seven groups today. Good luck."

We all applauded again. When Agnes came to our table she winked at us. "Good luck, guys. I'm rooting for you." She touched my cheek. "Enjoy your first pub quiz."

It was a sweet gesture that made me smile. "Thank you." She didn't know me that well and yet she had been nothing but kind to me. She was definitely a special lady.

"First thing we need is a name," Pavani said. "The stranger, the better."

Oh, I liked her thinking. "I see. What was it last time?"

"Know It Ales," Joe said, chuckling. "I came up with that one."

I grinned. "That's a good one."

"But you should come up with our name this time," Ian said. "Since it's your first time."

"Okay." *Think puns.* "What about Risky Quizness?"

"That's a really good one," Ian said.

"Yeah, write that one down." Pavani put her arm around me. "See, she's an excellent addition."

Agnes returned to the microphone she had placed on the bar and like that, the pub quiz had started.

"Question number one," Agnes said. "How did Carl Briggs end up naked in his own pond last summer?"

"Oh, I know this one," Ian said.

We all leaned forward so nobody could eavesdrop while Agnes repeated the question. It was too loud for anyone to overhear us, but better safe than sorry, I suppose. This was my first pub quiz and I felt motivated to win.

"Carl had just gotten a new barbeque and was trying it out for the first time. Things didn't really go as planned and he accidentally set his shorts on fire. He was shirtless at the time, so he shook off his shorts and underwear and even though he was fine at that point, he jumped into his own pond. His wife is still upset with him."

I laughed. "Really? Did he ever use his barbeque again?"

"Good question," Ian said.

"I'm sure he does," Ignacius said. "He boasts about the bloody thing every time I see him. Granted, I've never been invited to see it in action."

Agnes was getting ready for the second question, so I quickly scribbled down the answer.

"Question number two," she said. "Despite everything that she eats, has Betty ever thrown up? And if so, what was the situation?"

"I think we all know this one," Joe said as he glanced around the table.

Pavani chuckled. "I still laugh about it sometimes."

"There are some children that are still traumatised," Ignacius said, shaking his head.

"So she did?" I asked.

Marilyn leaned forward so she could see me. "It was during Halloween. She started chasing all the kids with their treats. She gobbled loads of bags and their contents until she started bleating and hobbling about in circles. I was on duty and I arrived just in time to see her throw up on Agnes's shoes."

"And it seemed like she couldn't stop. She vomited all over the place," Pavani said, wiping away tears from laughter. "It was like a horror film."

"Those poor kids," I said, but a bigger part of me was struggling not to laugh. I checked the answer sheet. Twenty-three questions to go. This was going to be interesting.

Chapter Twenty-One
Big Jimmy

IT WAS AROUND TEN O'CLOCK when all the teams' answers had been checked and Agnes was ready to read out the winning group. I had learned my fair share of stories and we had been able to fill out most answers but not all. We had a decent shot at winning.

I had switched from wine to iced tea since I wanted to be ready for tonight. The way things were looking, I would be able to leave earlier than I thought. It meant I could check out the club before finding out where they held their poker games. I would also need to bring money, which meant I had to dip into my savings account, but I was also confident that I could win. Any profit I'd make I could send to my mum.

This village was pleasant and quiet, and I liked that, but I realised I had also missed the thrill and excitement that came with conning.

"In third place with nineteen correct questions is the group Ales Well That Ends Well."

Everyone applauded as the group waved and laughed.

"That's also a funny name," Ignacius said. "As you can see, we all take the pub quiz quite seriously." He winked at me.

"In second place with twenty-four questions right is the group Risky Quizzness," Agnes announced and the rest of the pub applauded.

"We got second place, yes!" I excitedly clapped my hands. Ian chuckled.

"We did really well." Ignacius clasped Ian on his back.

"It's because of our new teammates," Marilyn said.

I wasn't even disappointed about not winning. We got all questions but one right. That was pretty cool. Not that I had contributed much apart from our name. But how could I? The point was for me to get to know more about the village, and I had.

"First place, with all questions right, including the trick question, is the group Mind Over Batter!" Agnes shouted and we all applauded a little louder.

One person walked up to Agnes to receive the small trophy and held it up for a few seconds so we could finish applauding.

"Alright, that was it for our pub quiz. Thank you so much for joining and enjoy the rest of your night," Agnes said. This also received a round of applause and then everything went back to normal.

"Wow, that was really fun," I said and stretched my arms. "You know, I'm exhausted. I really want to stay longer but my bed is calling me."

Ian checked his watch. "Yeah, I'm tired too. I'll walk with you."

I swallowed and felt the eyes of the rest of the group on me. "Yeah, sure." What else could I say?

Ian got up and so did I. "I had fun, guys. Thanks so much for inviting me."

"Anytime, dear." Pavani reached over and grabbed my hand. "Sleep well."

"You too."

I glanced at Ian. "Let me say bye to Agnes."

"Of course."

Agnes was behind the bar and smiled from ear to ear when we approached. "Did you enjoy the pub quiz? Sorry you didn't win, but you guys did really well."

"Thanks so much for all the fun questions. I enjoyed learning about all the crazy shenanigans that took place in this village."

"I figured you would appreciate it. Betty isn't the only unusual one."

I nearly snort-laughed but maintained a poker face. "I have noticed."

"Do you want new drinks?" she asked.

"No, I'm off to bed," I said.

"Yeah, I'm leaving as well," Ian added.

A twinkle appeared in her differently coloured eyes. "Interesting."

I rolled my eyes. "It's not like that. Ian, tell her."

"Tell her what?"

"That it's not like that," I said through gritted teeth.

"Like what?"

I glared at him. "Alright, I'm off." I stuck my tongue out at Agnes and she threw her head back and laughed.

"Have fun, kids."

I stomped off towards the double doors. Once through them, the cosy background sounds from the pub faded to silence. Ian followed me into the hallway.

"Did you have fun?" he asked.

"I did. Did you?"

"Yes. I think I might join the pub quiz more often." His eyes searched mine, and I found it difficult to look away.

I just nodded and edged closer to the stairs.

"Anyway," he said, "I'll see you around." His lips were pulled into a smile.

"Yes, I'll see you. Have a nice night." I started up the stairs, wanting to say more but the words would not leave my lips. It was probably for the best. Besides, I had more important things to focus on.

I closed all the curtains as soon as I entered my flat. I didn't want Ian to be able to see what I was doing, nor was anyone allowed to see me leave, or they might ask questions. The outfit I had laid out on my bed was designed to make anyone at the poker game tonight underestimate me. Everyone had a first impression when meeting someone, and outfits were an easy way to manipulate that impression.

I put on a short black dress with a low neckline. I didn't own high heels so I just wore my sneakers, which I figured only added to the vibe I was going for. My lipstick was black and I went heavy on the eyeliner. I wore my auburn hair down and finished the outfit off with my leather jacket. If I'd had jewellery, I would have put on several necklaces, but I didn't have anything like that. It was probably because my mother was obsessed with jewellery. She spent pretty much most of the money we made with cons on new necklaces or bracelets. Even though we travelled light, she had one special backpack for just her jewellery.

It took me about half an hour to get ready. Next would be sneaking out. I didn't want Agnes or Ian to see me leave. I didn't look like my usual self and it's not like many people here went clubbing. They would have questions. And I didn't want to answer those until I knew for sure whether or not this outing was worth it. In terms of information, that is. If I could win some money, it would be valuable either way.

I turned off all the lights to my flat and went into my bedroom to peek through the curtain and make sure Ian wasn't on his balcony. The doors were open but the light wasn't on in his bedroom and he wasn't there. Perhaps he had opened it to let his bedroom air, or perhaps he was getting tea before looking out into the alley. Not that it was very interesting, but he did have that fox, Lola, he liked.

Either way, it was now or never.

I grabbed my wallet, car keys, and a small black handbag that was big enough for me to put cash in. Agnes would still be busy in the pub, so it was doubtful she'd come into the private section, but still I kept my eyes and ears open as I hurried down the stairs. I opened the door that led to the alley and poked my head to make sure Ian still wasn't at his balcony. He wasn't.

I took a deep breath and closed the door behind me. My footfalls sounded on the pavement as I dashed out of the alley and ran towards the parking space where I had parked my Suzuki. My car sputtered and rattled as it came to life. If cars could have asthma, mine had it. I put my phone in my phone holder, turned on the navigation and went on my way.

HOT STUFF DIDN'T HAVE a queue, but it did have a lot of people outside chatting and smoking. I felt incredibly uneasy with the amount of money I had in my handbag. This whole thing was very risky, but I was good at poker and I needed to know if my employer was a murderer. Not just to gain the trust of the neighbourhood watch and Ian, but also for my own sake.

The music was a mixture of techno and hip hop and there were plenty of people dancing. Some were jumping up and down, others swaying their hips and grinding up against each other. It was not my thing. It never had been. Groups of friends were chatting at the bar or on the leather sofas in the back. My eyes scanned for a.... ah, there. A man in a suit was guarding double doors at the end of the bar.

My first order of business was getting a drink. I ordered a rum and coke and remained at the bar. To my relief, nobody hit on me. That was the last thing I needed. I was too impatient, though, to finish my entire drink, and I strutted over. I held my nose up high and as soon as I approached the bulky man by the doors, I pulled down my dress. My neckline was dangerously close to hitting my belly button but a girl had to do what a girl had to do. It was vital they underestimated me.

I studied my nails as I came to a stop in front of him.

"Can I help you?" he shouted over the music.

I raised an eyebrow and looked up at him. In my head I counted to three before I responded. I wanted him to be slightly on edge. Then I leaned forward so I could talk into his ear without having to raise my voice. If it meant he got a better look at my cleavage, so be it.

"I want to play," I said.

His gaze lingered on my chest before returning to my face. "Password?"

Password. Oh, boy.

I leaned forward again. "20K." He didn't have to know I had that on me. But he would never let his boss pass on the opportunity to win that amount of money.

He looked me up and down, perhaps because he couldn't believe it. It made me nervous which is why I studied my nails again. I needed him to think I'd just go elsewhere and wouldn't care either way.

I wasn't sure what their normal amounts were, perhaps twenty thousand pounds was nothing for them, but considering how small this city was, I figured it would be good enough.

He shifted his weight, then took a step back and opened the door for me.

I blew him a kiss and sashayed through the door. Things were only getting more exciting from here on out. My body tingled.

The hallway led to a bathroom on the right side and on the other side the area with all the poker games. There were about six tables with people—mostly men—playing different kinds of poker games. There was a jukebox in the corner playing slow songs and there was a bar. At the far end of the room was another door which was probably Big Jimmy's office, though I couldn't be sure.

Most eyes were on me when I entered, but that was probably because I was new and not because of my dress. The best way to observe everyone in this room was to go to the bar first. I needed to figure out what table to sit at. Big Jimmy was probably in his office and I'd have to find a way to draw his attention. Winning, of course, would be a good way.

The bartender had a shaved head with tattoos in his neck. His eyes were friendly and he grinned as I walked up to the bar.

"Never seen you here before," he said as his eyes scanned my body. "What can I get you?"

"It's my first time, so that would be correct. And a vodka, please."

"Going all out, I see. Very daring of you." He smiled.

"I am indeed daring." I twirled a strand of my hair. "And yeah, this is my first time here."

The bartender turned his back to me to grab the vodka and a glass. He poured the drink in front of me. "How did you hear about this place?"

This would be a great way to get some information. Bartenders knew a lot.

"From a bloke called Nathan," I said.

He eyed me. "The rich bloke? Well, not-so-rich bloke."

Aha.

"Yep, that's him."

The man handed me my drink. "He certainly likes to have ladies fix his mistakes."

We were getting somewhere already.

"Ah, yeah. You're talking about Harriet. She was crushing on him hard. But don't worry, I'm not here to help that guy out."

"Good. A real man fixes his own mess."

I smiled. "Did Harriet ever succeed in winning his money back? I never found out."

The bartender chuckled. "She was never here to win his money back, not with poker anyway. She knew some people here, that's all. She was trying to do odd jobs in order to get rid of his debt." He shakes his head. "I hope you're not friends with him."

Wait, she knew people? People like Big Jimmy? I was not expecting that. Did she have a criminal background? Ian would probably know.

"I'm not. Knowing him is unfortunate enough. But at least he gave me this tip. I like playing poker." I took a sip of my drink. It was a strong one, but I didn't mind.

"Then you're at the right place. Just make sure you know how to pay your debts."

"Oh, I only play to win." I winked at him.

Chapter Twenty-Two
Bluffing

I HAD JOINED ONE OF the poker tables with a virgin Pina Colada; I wanted to keep my wits about me. At the table were two other men and one woman. One was wearing sunglasses inside, so he was clearly bad at bluffing. The other man was wearing a suit and had grey streaks in his dark hair. The woman wore a burgundy outfit and expensive earrings. Not as expensive as my clients', though. She had probably earned some money playing poker and spent it on jewellery she otherwise couldn't afford. It reminded me of my mother.

If Harriet had come here to work a few side hustles, she could have gotten in over her head. Perhaps she'd witnessed something and Big Jimmy wanted her silenced. Or maybe she'd made a mistake. I also wondered if her boyfriend had noticed her being gone at night then. How often had she come here to make more money and trim Nathan's debt?

It would explain why Nathan had been stringing her along. She was actually doing something valuable for him.

I had to talk with Big Jimmy, even if it was risky. It meant I had to stand out and I would if I had a few winning streaks. We were playing Texas Hold 'em. I just had to pay attention and start off being cautious. It was important to first find out the other players' tells. I also had to pay attention to the cards that were being dealt and how many were left.

I soon found out Sunglasses touched his nose when he was bluffing, whereas Suit licked his lips. Earrings was a bit trickier, but when she tucked a strand of her blond hair behind her ears, she had good cards, I realised. That was equally helpful.

It took me two rounds before I started winning, much to their dismay. And I kept on winning until they didn't want to play with me anymore. Internally, I squealed with pleasure. I had won five thousand pounds in just a few rounds. It wasn't that much, considering the table in the back was raising with a lot of bills. They had to be the big players, which meant I had to make it to their table if I wanted Big Jimmy's attention.

I went to the next table and played Blackjack. I lost twice before winning three times and then returned to the bar.

"It looks like it's your lucky day," the bartender said as he made me another virgin Pina Colada.

"It makes for a nice change," I said as I glanced at the table at the back near Big Jimmy's office.

The bartender followed my gaze. "I wouldn't go there, if I were you. They play with big money and don't like to lose. And when they're not happy, Big Jimmy isn't happy. Especially if it involves someone new who's been winning all night."

"Yes, I imagine Big Jimmy doesn't lose, even when he does lose."

His eyebrows shot up. "Exactly." He handed me my drink.

"Don't worry. I don't lose either." I downed the drink and gave him a confident smile. He probably thought I had a death wish.

I joined another table where the stakes were about similar to the previous game. If I wanted to gain the attention of Big Jimmy, or even the high rollers, I needed to make a lot of money. This group was easy enough to figure out. I lost two rounds, but then I started winning.

Three times I won before I decided to move on to the next table. Also, because my opponents were getting crankier by the second. That was good, though. It would mean word would spread faster and it wouldn't be long until something would happen.

It was risky, though. There was definitely the possibility for a newbie like me to actually reach the bigger players, but it would be to test me and make sure I wasn't cheating. It would also mean that winning would get me in a lot of trouble. But so would losing. It really was a tricky situation. But my goal wasn't necessarily all my winnings. My goal was information.

Once you figure out what someone wants and how far they're willing to go for it, manipulation becomes easy.

Jimmy wanted money and to maintain his status. I could work with that.

I lost only once at the next table, and then won twice. The stack of bills was getting harder to fit into my handbag and I was starting to feel giddy about it. So much money. I hadn't seen this much since I...well, since my conning days.

Things were going well, but it was also getting later. I wanted to hurry things along and get some answers.

I took a deep breath and didn't even bother getting more liquid courage. I put an extra swing in my step as I approached the table close to Big Jimmy's office.

They were all men and the money that was on the table was more than I'd seen at the previous ones. I raised an eyebrow as if to be unimpressed, but said nothing.

I simply waited for them to be finished. It was clear they were nearly done. Two men—one with a short beard and turban and one with a handlebar moustache and a cowboy hat—were left with cards in their hands and they were trying to out-bluff each other.

That left a man in a high-end business suit and an old guy, Joe old, who had a cold expression in his eyes as he stared at me.

"What do you want?" he asked.

I shrugged. "Just watching until I can join."

"Sweetheart, the big boys are playing. This ain't for you," the cowboy said in an American accent.

"I'm not your sweetheart and you guys aren't big boys, judging by the way you are playing."

They all looked up at me at that. I noticed the adjoining table became quiet and tension rose.

"But I get it. You're intimidated because of all that money I've been winning ever since I got here. You'd rather stick with the people whose tells you already know." I smiled sweetly.

His handlebar moustache twitched.

"I guess I'll take all my winnings and go, then." I studied my nails as if they were more interesting than that table and started to turn away.

"Hang on now, sweetheart. If you're gonna talk to us like that, we might as well teach you a lesson." He threw his cards on the table and leaned forward to the man in the turban. "Royal Flush."

The other guys made noises to show they were impressed while the guy with the turban threw his cards on the table and muttered a curse.

"Loser buys us drinks," the old man said and clapped him on the shoulder.

"And that means you're in, sweetheart," the cowboy said.

"Alright then." I didn't sound too impressed.

"I'm Ricky," he continued. "That sore loser over there is Arjun." He pointed at the guy in the turban, then at the old man. "That's George, and next to him is Craig."

The man in the suit barely paid me any attention, but George was studying me without shame. His eyes lingered a bit too long on my cleavage, but that was good. I needed them to underestimate me.

Since I had seen two of them play already, I knew Arjun's tell. I had to admit Ricky was more difficult to read, and I had yet to see the others in action. This was going to be interesting.

When Arjun returned with whisky for everyone, including me, we started. The first two rounds I folded early as not to lose too much money, and I made sure I had a tell. It was the smallest lip twitch and I knew they'd all pick up on it. They were trained to.

"Not doing so hot, are you, sweetheart?" Ricky asked with a grin as we started the third round.

"I always need some warming up, but Lady Luck is on my side."

"That's funny, I always say she's on my lap." George laughed.

Okay, then. Charming image.

I actually had good cards. So I revealed my tell, and called it so I could keep my hand and keep playing. Arjun folded. It left the four of us in the next round. This time Ricky raised. It was a lot of money. Craig raised as well, which made me even more nervous. I mean, I had good cards, but I realised Ricky's tell for when he had a good hand as well. And he had one. Craig I wasn't sure about. He had an incredible poker face. This was risky. But I had to try.

George folded with a sigh and slouched off to the bar.

I realised that we had started to gather attention and some people had gathered around to look. This was good.

The next round Ricky raised again. He observed me as he did, but I was watching Craig from the corner of my eye. And there it was. The tiniest tap on the table. His cards weren't that good. The question of course was whether or not mine were better than Ricky.

I did the boldest thing ever.

I went all in. It was all my money. A person behind me gasped. There were murmurs.

We stared at each other.

Time seemed to tick on slowly.

"Call," he said.

"Four of a kind," I said as I put my cards down.

There was more murmuring.

Ricky narrowed his eyes at me and placed down his cards. My heart nearly stopped. A full house.

I smiled as I realised I had actually won.

People actually applauded.

"Thank you," I said gracefully. "That was a really exciting game. Thank you for playing," I said to Ricky.

He narrowed his eyes at me. "Are you stopping?"

I glanced at all the money on the table. I couldn't believe that was all mine now. Well, who knew what would be left after my chat with Big Jimmy? It would fit in my handbag, but barely.

"Actually, I have to have a little chat with someone here," I said as I started collecting the money.

"Who?" Ricky asked.

A very large man in a black suit appeared next to the table.

Ah, that had to be Big Jimmy.

"Him," I said.

BIG JIMMY'S OFFICE was actually quite cosy. There was a large bookcase, a globe that held liquor and a wooden desk with a painting of dogs playing poker behind it. It smelt like soap. I turned to Big Jimmy but he just left and shut the door behind him.

Okay, so that wasn't Big Jimmy.

Which meant... I turned back around to the desk. The chair was turned away from me and suddenly it whirled around, as if Big Jimmy was some sort of cartoon villain.

He was also a little person, which was why his head didn't pop out from behind his chair.

"Big Jimmy?" I asked.

"How good of you to know my name. Especially since it's your first time here," he said as he eyed me up and down. "I like your dress." He had black, curly hair and wore stylish glasses and a striped suit.

"Thanks. May I sit?" I indicated one of the armchairs in front of his desk.

He gave a curt nod.

I sat down and put my handbag on the floor. Clutching it to my chest was my first instinct, but I had to give him the impression that I didn't care much about money.

"How did you find this place? Or know my name?" he asked as he poured himself a cup of tea. It was a teapot decorated with flowers.

So far he was not what I thought he would be.

"I actually came here for a reason, and that's to talk to you about Harriet."

He glanced up at me, but that was the only reaction I got. He was also good at maintaining a poker face.

"That's interesting," he said.

"I'm guessing you called me in here because I've been winning. How about I ask you five questions about her that you have to answer truthfully, and in exchange I give you twenty percent of my winnings."

I knew he wouldn't accept twenty percent but starting low is always the smart thing to do.

He narrowed his eyes at me, then bent down to grab something.

Oh, oh. Was it a gun? I glanced around the room. The only exit was behind me and no doubt guarded by his associate. Why hadn't I told Ian where I'd been going?

Chapter Twenty-Three
Five Answers

WHEN BIG JIMMY CAME back up he was holding a tiny poodle. I raised my eyebrow in surprise.

"It's a Toy Poodle. Very small and cute, but extremely voracious. I've seen this one take down a Doberman."

The dog was staring at me with black, beady eyes. It did look cute.

It started growling.

Okay, maybe not so cute.

Big Jimmy smirked. "Now, since this is your first visit here I won't be too hard on you. I will answer your five questions, but in return I get eighty percent of your winnings."

"Fifty," I said. "Final offer. Unless you want me spreading rumours that you don't let people win fair and square. Will be bad for business, no?"

The dog growled again. It probably meant it could feel Big Jimmy's unease. Which was good. I stopped myself from smiling though. He was still a dangerous man.

"Fine," he said through gritted teeth. "But you are playing with fire."

"I know," I said in a cheerful tone and started counting the money in my purse while I lined up the first question I wanted to ask him.

"When was the last time you saw Harriet?" I glanced up because I wanted to see his reaction, but he was petting his dog.

"Last week. Friday night, I think." He scratched the poodle's chin.

Clearly he would not elaborate. He was going to answer my question and be short about it. "Why was she working for you?" Since the bartender already told me she was doing things for Big Jimmy, there was no point asking why she was here. He would probably answer that she was there to see him. Which would not be helpful, even if it was true.

At this, his lips pulled downwards.

"She wanted to pay off Nathan what's-his-face's debt."

Aha. There we go. Important confirmed info. It also meant I had to think carefully about my remaining questions. She was strangled and put in the boot of her car. It seemed a bit mafia-like, but the strangling seemed personal. Then again, it was possible that she and Big Jimmy went way back.

"How close were you with Harriet?"

He reached for his cup of tea and took a sip.

Did this mean he had to think about his answer? Was he buying himself time? I was assuming he would be a man of his word, but only because in his line of business it would be beneficial. Credibility was everything when you were trying to make a name for yourself in criminal circles. Or when maintaining it.

"She used to work for me, but quit when she got a boyfriend. He didn't like her work so she decided to go on the straight and narrow."

That had to be Dylan. He'd said he wanted to break up with her, maybe that was because he figured out she had been taking jobs from Big Jimmy again. Did he know she was doing it for Nathan?

"Did her boyfriend know anything about her working for you again or about Nathan?"

"Not that I know of," he replied.

Hmm. That's not really helpful.

"Last question." He took another sip of his tea.

I kept counting my money, because I didn't want to stay here after I had asked my final question. When I finished, I grabbed the stack and placed it on his desk. "Are you in any way responsible for Harriet's death?"

He looked me straight in my eyes. "No, and if I find out who did do it, they're going to meet the same fate as her."

Oh, that was surprising. So he did care for her.

"Now, get the hell out."

"Gladly. Thanks for your time." I got up, closed my handbag that had fifty percent of my winnings, and sashayed towards the door.

"And if you ever get tired of cleaning," he said, "you know where to find me."

I turned around but he was already focussed on his dog. That was also surprising. I hadn't expected him to say that. I guess he appreciated my guts. Or perhaps he was excited about the idea of using me to win back money for him from lucky patrons.

I opened the door. The man who had come to get me was nowhere to be seen. I held my chin up as I made my way to the door, though I did give the bartender a little wave. He grinned back at me. I made my way back through the grinding bodies on the dance floor and hurried to escape the loud music that was banging all the way in my bones.

In the meantime, my knuckles were white from clutching my handbag. Half of me was worried that someone would know and tackle me for it.

I made it out without any interruptions and the cool air was refreshing. There were people outside smoking and I hurried towards my car. I had to pass an alley in order to make it to the parking space.

At least this night was successful. I had won some information and mo—

Someone grabbed me and dragged me into the alley. Without thinking, I kicked his leg and then slammed my body into his, forcing him to hit the brick wall.

Ian grunted. "Wait, it's me," he said with a wheeze.

I looked up at his pained expression and backed up.

"Wow, I guess I don't have to worry about you." He rubbed his arm and glanced at me. "Ever played rugby?" His frown disappeared and he grinned at me.

I adjusted the strap of my bag. "Sorry, but you shouldn't drag a woman into an alley in the middle of the night. Hasn't being a detective taught you that at least?"

His eyes scanned my body as he realised what I was wearing. It was too dark to see if he was blushing, but I had the feeling he was.

He cleared his throat. "I didn't mean to scare you. I was just—I don't know, I figured you were doing something related to the case and didn't want anyone to see us together. But that's stupid because who would know I'm a detective? I guess I'm tired."

"You saw me leave?"

"Actually, Joe saw you leave. He's a creature of the night, I guess, and was just leaving the pub. He saw me on my balcony and begged me to follow you. He was worried."

"Because I looked like I was going clubbing?"

"No. Because he said you looked like you were acting like a spy as you made it to your car." Ian grinned.

I chuckled. "That does sound about right."

His grin disappeared. "What were you thinking? Big Jimmy is not someone to mess with. How did you even know about him?"

I shrugged, then shivered as it was getting cold. "I'm a maid. I have my ways."

Ian took off his jacket and threw it over my shoulders. "Come on, let's get home. We'll talk about it there." He walked me to my car.

"Mine is over there," he said and pointed to his red Mini Cooper. "I'll follow you."

"You have a cute car. Which is good, because I can't drive."

His eyebrow went up.

"I may have had a few tiny drinks." I blinked innocently.

He sighed. "Alright. I can't wait to hear what happened tonight. Let's go." He put his hand on my lower back as he escorted me to his car. His hand felt nice there.

We didn't speak until we were in his Mini Cooper. He immediately turned on the heating. "What would you have done if I hadn't been here?"

"I would have made it to my car and then called for a taxi," I said.

He sighed. "And what was the reason for your visit to Big Jimmy?"

"Harriet knew about Nathan's debt and she wanted to be with him. He, of course, was never planning to do that, but Harriet would have had hope. I figured she'd try to make herself valuable to him and help him. I went in there to play some poker and draw Big Jimmy's attention."

At this, Ian's nostrils flared.

"And then the bartender told me that Harriet had tried to do some odd jobs for Big Jimmy in order to help Nathan out with his debt."

"The bartender just told you this?"

"When I mentioned Nathan, he said something about another woman coming to his aid and pretty much told me Harriet wanted to lower the debt in return for odd jobs for her former boss."

"What? Harriet used to work for Big Jimmy?"

"Yep. Jimmy also confirmed it. He seems to care about her."

Ian shifted in his seat. "You talked to Big Jimmy?"

"I told you, that was my plan." I liked the flash of concern in his eyes.

"Go on."

"I played poker, won some games, got Big Jim's attention and he invited me into his office." I paused.

"Keep going," Ian said with impatience. His eyes scanned my face, neck and arms as if he was checking to make sure I wasn't harmed.

"I told him I wanted to ask him five questions and in return I'd pay him back a large portion of my winnings."

Ian bit his lip and ran a hand through his hair. "Why would you—do you—what were you thinking?"

"He agreed."

His head snapped in my direction. "Really?"

"Yes. And like I said, he seemed to care for her enough to be pissed off that she was murdered. She stopped working for him the first time because of Dylan. He didn't want her working for Big Jimmy."

Ian scoffed. "Smart guy."

"I also asked him if Big Jimmy was responsible for her murder in any way and he said no. I think he was telling the truth."

"You asked him that?" He inhaled slowly. "Did he hurt you?"

"No. Not at all. I think he respected my courage." I smiled at Ian.

He shook his head. "I don't like this at all."

"Why? He's bad news, but it would do him more harm than good if he went around physically hurting people for winning at his underground poker club. We made a deal. Money for information."

"Even so, please don't ever come back here."

"That worried, huh?"

Ian paused for a second as he stared at me. "Yes," he said.

"Okay, I won't then." I ignored the pleasant warmth that spread through my chest.

"Thanks." He started the engine and yawned. "Let's get home, then. And thanks for the information. It is helpful."

"I know. Big Jimmy could be a good liar, but I don't see him having a motive if Harriet was working for him. I doubt she would have stopped. Not unless she truly was breaking it off with Nathan. But even then, it wouldn't be a problem for Big Jimmy. He'd just continue going after Nathan." I leaned back and relaxed as Ian drove on.

"Could Dylan have found out that she was working for Jimmy again?" he mused.

"But surely that would have sparked a fight, not a murder?"

"You'd be surprised."

"If she had decided not to help Nathan, would he have been angry enough to kill her, you think?" I asked.

"I don't know. Unfortunately, people kill each other over the pettiest of things."

Chapter Twenty-Four
Sunday Funday

THE PUB WAS DARK WHEN we arrived at it. The entire village seemed deserted and was quiet. It felt like the whole world was asleep.

"I'll take you to your car tomorrow," Ian said as we got out of his.

I knew better than to argue. "Thanks, I appreciate it."

He followed me to the private entrance at the side of the pub. "So, I'm just curious...how much money did you win exactly?"

I turned the key in the lock and pushed open the door. "Enough," I said and turned back to him with a smile.

"And how did you get so good at poker?"

"Practice. Do you want to play sometime?"

A slow smile spread across his face. "Sure."

"Okay." I nodded and stepped inside. "Thanks for checking on me."

"Anytime. And you look really beautiful. Good night." He gave a hesitant wave.

Why did he have to be so cute? I waved back and then closed the door and sighed. It had been a long Saturday. Time for sleep.

THAT SUNDAY MORNING I slept in until ten o'clock. I had my toast and tea in bed, then showered and read for about an hour with the TV on in the background. Ian's flat looked empty, and I wondered when he would show up so we could get my car, but I was in no rush. This was going to be a relaxed Sunday, or, as my mother would always call it: Sunday Funday.

There was a knock on my door. Had Agnes let him in? My heartbeat sped up and I put down my e-reader to answer the door.

"Hi, love," Agnes said. Her rosy cheeks were glowing and she smiled at me. "We don't open until noon and I'm making a cheesecake. Do you want to help me? I figured it would be fun."

I tried to hide the disappointment I felt. "I see. If it's your morning off, are you sure you want to be baking?"

"Of course. I love making food. Besides, this cheesecake is easy as pie." She chuckled at her own joke.

Agnes was always so cheerful. I liked that about her. "Okay. I'll help." To be honest, I was kind of honoured to see her at work. She was such a good cook. Also, I'd always wanted to do something like this with my own mother. Perhaps when all this was over I could convince her to bake with me. Perhaps she would finally realise what mattered in life.

"Wonderful." She clasped my hand excitedly and then bounced down the stairs in anticipation. Her age didn't hold her back from anything.

I chuckled to myself and locked the door behind me before following her downstairs and into her private kitchen. She had already set up the ingredients and the radio was playing fifties songs in the background. Betty was bleating in the back garden and started a staring contest when she noticed me looking at her. I had to break it off because Agnes handed me an apron with kittens on it.

"Thanks," I said and put it on. "I don't think I've ever worn one. Other than the one for my maid's outfit."

"Most people don't wear them anymore, I think. But it's just handy when you're as messy as I am when cooking. I swear, stuff gets everywhere. Especially tomato sauce. It's out to ruin my clothes."

I studied the ingredients. Cream cheese, lots of sugar, gluten-free biscuits, a lemon, and eggs.

"We're going to make a gluten-free cheesecake. The biscuits are going to be the bottom, then the cream cheese mixed with the sugar, lemon and eggs are going to be the cheesecake itself. The powdered sugar goes on top. It's lovely. It needs to go in the oven for an hour, but it's worth the wait."

"Alright. Do we get to eat afterwards?"

She gaped at me. "Of course! Cake is to be eaten."

"Well, I just thought maybe it was for the pub or something," I said.

"No, no. Everything made in this kitchen is for me and my friends." She winked as if to say that included me.

I felt my cheeks warm. "Alright, let's get started then." My hands were itching. And my mouth was watering in anticipation.

She instructed me to put the biscuits in the machine and grind them to crumbs along with the melted butter. It made a lot of noise but was satisfying to do. Then I patted them down on the bottom of the cake tin while Agnes started mixing the cream cheese and sugar.

"Do you have any big cookers in your family?"

"No. It's always been me and my mother and she never cooks."

"Ah. I'm sorry to hear that. Cooking in my family was always something of a bonding experience, I suppose you can call it. At the end of a long day we all got together and pitched in. My younger sister would always help set the table, while my oldest sister cut vegetables. I usually stirred a sauce. My dad would pour us all drinks and take care of the meat. It was always very cosy."

Her family sounded warm and loving. "And when you were with your husband? Did you maintain that tradition?"

"Oh, yes. We always cooked together. He would always follow my instructions and let me take the lead."

"I bet that was a smart decision," I said.

She laughed. "It was. When we first met, he always burnt toast. But I taught him well. And even though we remained a small family, we were still a family." Her tone got sadder.

I didn't like it when she was sad. "I'm glad you had such a loving husband."

She looked up and flashed me a smile. "Me too. He was the best. But the family I have now is great as well."

"You mean the neighbourhood watch?"

"Yes. They are the best bunch. I know they can be a bit odd sometimes, but that's why I love them so much. One time Marilyn and I took a walk in the park and there were three horrible male ducks that were terrorising a family with young kids and when I went to help them—you know I have a way with unusual animals—they attacked me."

"Ducks attacked you?" My eyes widened.

"Oh, yes. They can be vicious. But Marilyn, bless her heart, she just jumped in without hesitation, despite her phobia. It was amazing."

"Really? She did that?"

Agnes nodded so hard that her curly hair bounced. "They are all good people and they've all lost something or someone. I think that's why we are extra good to each other. We know what it feels like."

"That makes sense."

"But don't feel intimidated by the fact that we all know each other longer. We are very glad that you are part of the gang, so to speak."

"I-I'm part of the gang?" I looked up from what I was doing.

"Of course you are. You're lovely. Now, when that's done, wash your hands and I'll let you put the rest in. It's almost done already."

I didn't say anything, because I was afraid I'd cry if I would. I blinked away upcoming tears and washed my hands.

Agnes watched as I stirred in the remaining ingredients and then I poured it into the cake tin. We smoothed it out together, then licked the special knife we used for it and put the cake in the oven.

"Good job, partner," she said and held up her hand.

"Good job." I gave her a high five.

"Now, sit. I'll make us a nice cup of tea."

I sat down at the breakfast table and looked out into the garden again. Betty was gone. I was about to tell Agnes when Betty's head popped up above the window sill. I nearly fell off my chair. Agnes didn't even notice since the kettle was making noise.

I glared at Betty through the window. It seemed like we were back to our staring contest. At least it was better than her stalking the cobbled streets, looking for unwitting pieces of clothing.

"There we go," Agnes said after a moment and put down a floral teapot and two cups. When I glanced back at Betty, she was at the back of the garden, grazing like nothing had happened.

I wasn't even surprised anymore.

"So, if you don't mind me gossiping with you ... how is it going with you and Ian? And please, do tell me if it's none of my business. I'm only asking because I want you both to be happy. And I can keep a secret." She zipped her lips as if to prove it.

Agnes seemed sincere and was very friendly, but it didn't necessarily mean I could trust her. My mother was proof of that. Heck, any con artist was proof of that.

"He is a wonderful man. It's just that I'm not sure I want a relationship. I'm not even sure how long I'll be staying."

She was about to put her tea cup to her lips, but froze. "Really? Do you think you'll be leaving soon?"

I shifted in my seat. So far I'd only told Ian and clearly he hadn't told anyone. "Well, my mother is ill and I just want to make as much money as I can in a short amount of time and then go back to her. She needs the money for this experimental treatment." It was not a lie. And a big part of me wanted them to know that at least. In case they found out why I was here.

The money I had won yesterday was already helpful, but it would only cover the plane ticket. For the treatment costs, I still needed to work my magic.

"Oh, love. I'm so sorry." She put her hand on mine and squeezed. "I had no idea. What a terrible burden. Is there anything I can do? Maybe we can do some sort of fundraiser?"

I felt tears well up again. "No, no. Please. It's my problem. Besides, I really don't want your hard-earned money."

"Even so, this is terrible. You're forced to be apart from your mother in order to help her out. It's a lot of pressure on you, not to mention unfair that you can't spend time with her."

That was how I felt, but it didn't matter. I had to do what needed to be done. "It's just the way things are. Please, don't worry about it. I didn't mean to bring down the mood."

"What? You did no such thing. We are getting to know each other. Besides, when you're friends, your friends' problems are your own. Isn't that how it is?"

I smiled. I wouldn't know. I never really had any. But I was beginning to understand.

"Seriously, don't worry about it. I've gotten some new clients now that—Sorry, that sounds horrible."

"Now that Harriet is dead? Yes, well, that is simply a fact. Besides, it's not like you knew her. We didn't even know her well. It's a small village, but we don't know everybody."

"Even so. I didn't mean to make it sound like her death was beneficial to me."

"I know, pet. You've been working hard and word-of-mouth will mean that you'll get even more clients. Besides, most wealthy people give their help large Christmas bonu—ah, you'll probably be gone by then."

I nodded. "That is the plan." Three months, tops. I really didn't want to spend any more time on this con.

"Wow. I will miss you so much."

"Agnes, really. Don't think about it. Who knows what will happen?"

"Does Ian know?"

I nodded. "Yeah, I told him about my mother and that I'm not planning to stay long."

"I see. I was really rooting for you guys. Long distance works for some people, you know?"

"I know," I said with a laugh. "Like I said, who knows what will happen?"

Chapter Twenty-Five
Cheesecake

AGNES WAS IN THE MIDDLE of telling me a story about her holiday to Spain where she and her husband accidentally ventured onto a nudist beach, when the doorbell rang.

"I wonder who that is," Agnes said as she got up.

A moment later Ian stood in the kitchen.

"Hey," he said. "What smells so nice?"

"We've been baking. It's gluten-free cheesecake." She opened the oven door to give him a peek.

"Oh, nice. How long does it have to stay in the oven?"

"Forty more minutes."

"That's perfect. I'll take Clara to pick up her car and by the time we return, we can all have a slice." He winked at me.

"Sounds good to me."

"Wait, wait. Why do you have to pick up your car?"

"How about we share that when we get back? It's kind of a long story," I said.

"Okay, I'll make sure there's more tea by the time you get back."

"Thanks."

"We won't be long," Ian added and put his hand on my lower back as he escorted me out of the kitchen. Didn't he know it kind of drove me insane when he did that?

"Did you sleep well?" he asked as we stepped outside. The sun was hidden behind clouds and it was a bit chilly.

"I did. Did you?"

"So you didn't dream of scary guys pulling you into an alley? What a relief."

"Of course not. It's not like I was pulled into an alley by a scary guy."

"Oh, no? I'm not scary?"

I shook my head. "You're as harmless as a sleeping kitten."

At this, he laughed. It was a pleasant sound. "I don't think anyone has ever compared me to a sleeping kitten before."

"Good. Then I'm the first. I feel special."

He grabbed my arm, forcing me to stop just as we had reached his Mini Cooper. All humour had vanished from his face. "You are special," he said. "Look, I'm sorry I was so worried yesterday. I'm actually very impressed by what you did. You're pretty, err, cool."

I felt myself blush. Nobody had ever called me that. "Th—thanks. That's very sweet of you."

"I mean it."

Before the rest of my body started blushing—was that even possible?—I walked to the passenger's side of the car.

Luckily he didn't say anything else, and we got in and drove back to Hot Stuff. It looked different in daylight and there seemed to be no one around. Ian waited until I got in my car and drove off, then followed me. Was he being polite or protective? My ex had never been either of those things. He had never treated me badly or anything, but he'd never done anything swoon-worthy. Ian had, and we weren't even dating.

Did that say something about our connection or simply about what kind of man Ian was?

Things would have been so much easier if all these people weren't so genuinely welcoming. Agnes told me I was part of the club even though we still barely knew each other. They were all trusting and friendly, not suspicious in the least. Which, yes, of course was good for me, but it also made it all harder.

Then again, it wasn't like I was doing this for a bad or selfish reason.

I bit my lip. That didn't matter. I was going to have to leave these people. Without notice, without warning. And that would be hard.

"YOU REALLY DID THAT?" Agnes asked when all three of us were enjoying a slice of cooled-off cheesecake with powdered sugar on top.

I nodded. "Yeah. Though Ian makes it sound more exciting than it was."

"No way. I think you're underselling it. What you did was very impressive."

"I can't believe you went undercover just to get a few answers. And I can't believe you actually got them from a man like Big Johnny."

"Big Jimmy," Ian and I said simultaneously.

She waved her hand as if to dismiss her mistake. "This is interesting, though. Do you think Dylan found out she was working for him again?"

"I don't know. Last time I saw him he was upset at the thought that he'd wanted to break up with her. Maybe he did find out and was planning on ending things. I don't think Harriet would have minded. It seemed she was quite serious about Nathan."

"Which brings us back to Nathan," Agnes said. "He was clearly just using Harriet."

"But why kill the person who's helping you get rid of your debt?"

"Unless maybe she realised he was using her and decided not to help. Maybe she threatened him. You know, bad mouth him to Big Johnny or even tell Pearl about everything."

I ignored her mistake this time and nodded. "It is possible. Why put her in her car and dump it in the lake?"

Ian was perfectly fine just eating his cheesecake as he let us speculate. I was sure the cogs in his mind were turning and that he registered everything we were saying.

"To make sure her body wasn't found, of course," Agnes said. "The letter that was printed must have been to throw everybody off her scent."

"Hmm. It might also mean that she died away from home. She must have driven to someone and then gotten killed. Let's say she was killed at Nathan's house, then obviously he'd want her car out of sight and get rid of her body. Also, her blood was in one of the bathrooms."

"But the letter was typed on her computer, and she had been researching poisons." Agnes tapped her finger against her lips. "When I open the pub, you should all come in for lunch. We can discuss the case again."

At this, Ian chuckled.

"What?" Agnes asked.

He shook his head. "You sound like private detectives."

She winked at me. "We kind of are."

I smiled.

"Look, I know I asked for your help when we found the letter, but now that it's officially a homicide and I'm on the case, I don't really need you guys to get involved. In fact, I think I'd prefer it if you guys didn't. Someone is a murderer and if they're willing to kill Harriet, they're certainly willing to kill any of you." There was clear tension in his shoulders as he said this.

"We're just talking in a pub, that's all." Agnes flashed him an innocent smile.

"Right." He finished his cheesecake. "This was delicious."

"Clara did most of the work."

I felt myself blush. "No, not really. I'm not good at anything kitchen related."

"Are you kidding?" Agnes's voice was higher than usual as she reached forward and put her hand on mine. "This was your first cheesecake and you nailed it. Well done."

I looked down. "Thanks."

"If this was your first cheesecake, I'm looking forward to what else you're going to make," Ian said.

All these compliments were too much, really.

"Alright. I should start setting up things next door. You guys just relax here and I'll see you soon." She got up and while humming a tune, she left the kitchen.

It left me and Ian alone.

"Thanks again for helping me get my car back."

"No worries. Next time you're going undercover, please tell me. It would make me feel better."

I nodded.

He cleared his throat and rubbed his arm. "Err, listen. I know maybe we didn't get off on the best foot, but I like spending time with you."

I started sweating.

"Do you maybe want to go on a date sometime?"

"I—I think it's best if we don't. I am not here to stay long, remember?"

He pressed his lips into a straight line. "Right. And you don't want to get too attached."

"Exactly. My mother needs me. So... I would like to be friends, though."

His eyes creased as he smiled. "Of course. I would like that too." He opened his mouth to say something else, but then closed it.

"I'll be in the pub all day, probably, so maybe I'll see you there?"

He nodded.

I got up and brushed my lips against his cheek. Before he could see me blush even more, I rushed out of the kitchen and dashed upstairs.

Still, this had been the right thing to say. I could probably handle being friends with him. It would all be okay.

Chapter Twenty-Six
An Arrest?

I STAYED UPSTAIRS AND tidied up my flat before going down to the pub at lunchtime. I realised I was actually looking forward to seeing the neighbourhood watch gang.

Pavani, Joe, and Marilyn were already at our usual table by the window. They all greeted me with smiles and were engaged in conversation.

"And then the woman told me she wanted to report her cat missing," Marilyn said. "So I told her we only dealt with missing people and suggested she could hang up posters and check the local shelters. But she demanded we arrange a search party for her slightly overweight tabby."

Pavani shook her head. "Poor woman."

"She's not a poor woman. She was a bloody nuisance," Marilyn said. Since she was usually soft-spoken, this woman had clearly driven her up the wall.

"I know," Pavani said, "but imagine how empty her life must be if she is that obsessed with her cat. I feel bad for her."

Marilyn huffed and crossed her arms. "Well, she didn't care that much when I threatened her with a lawsuit."

Joe chuckled. "Was she short with blue eyeshadow?"

"Yeah, how do you know?"

"She lives behind me. She has four cats and each time one of them stays out longer than two hours, she's convinced they've been hit by a car. I believe she dresses up the cats as well. Her cats are usually having fun in the park by the church, so I'm certain they'll make it back home."

"This happened today?" I asked Marilyn.

"Yes. I sometimes have to work the weekend shift. It alternates. I don't mind, though. I only mind when people try to waste my time. I've got plenty of paperwork, you know?"

"I can imagine."

Pearl walked up to our table, looking beautiful as ever. She had soup, a panini, and a chicken sandwich on her tray. She put down the soup for Pavani, the panini for Joe, and the chicken sandwich for Marilyn.

"There you go. Now, Clara. What can I get you?"

"Hey, Pearl." I had already forgotten she worked here. "Err, I'd like a tuna sandwich and a tea, please."

"No problem." She flashed me her white teeth and was off again.

"It's going to be difficult to talk about the case with her around," Joe said as he stared after her.

"Do we have any news?" Pavani asked.

"Agnes said you had something to share," Marilyn said as she looked at me.

Right. The Big Jimmy thing. "I do, but we should probably wait until everyone's here and until we're sure Pearl won't be at our table anytime soon."

"Good point." Marilyn nodded. "But it's Sunday, so Ignacius will be here around dinner time."

"Ah. I'll tell you after Pearl brings me my sandwich, then."

"In the meantime, we can talk about you and Ian," Pavani said with a wink. "Did you guys do anything special when he walked you up after the pub quiz?"

"You guys really love gossip, huh?" I raised my eyebrow.

"It's not gossip. I have no love life, you see? I need to live vicariously." She laughed.

A smile tugged on my lips. "Trust me, there's nothing to be found here. My love life is non-existent."

Pavani nudged me. "Things can change."

I really hoped not.

After Pearl had brought me my lunch, I told the gang about my visit to Big Jimmy.

Joe actually put down his chicken sandwich. "You just went in there? On your own? Without telling anyone?"

I shrugged. "He's not some serial killer. He just runs an underground poker club."

"He's a thug by the sounds of it. And for all you know he is a killer," Joe said, shaking his head.

"It worked out just fine. I know what I'm doing."

"You really have a way with people if you made that deal with Big Jimmy like that," Pavani said with admiration.

"I just adopted a role. Like acting," I said.

"Interesting." Pavani nodded. "It was a clever way to get information."

"More like risky," Joe added with a grunt.

"I'm just saying," she said to him, "it's quite smart. We've never thought to do it. We've always just relied on gossip and walking around the neighbourhood, like when people's socks got stolen from clothes lines."

"People's socks got stolen from clothes lines?" I asked.

Marilyn waved a hand. "It turned out to be the mayor, sleepwalking."

Wow, never a dull moment in this village.

"Do you think we could do some undercover work in order to find out who killed Harriet?" Pavani asked.

I tapped my chin. "I think the next step is to find out if the boyfriend knew about her extracurricular activities. Which could actually involve some undercover work."

Pavani wiggled her eyebrows. "Go on."

"I don't know if he has seen you guys before, but some of us could pretend to work for Big Jimmy and confront Dylan."

"I'm in," Pavani immediately said.

"I think it would be best if Ignacius and Joe went."

"What?" Pavani's grin disappeared.

"Wait, what? Me?" Joe asked, his eyes wide.

"Yeah. Two men in leather jackets is what would fit the stereotypical image, so it's what we will give him." Even if Joe looked like someone's friendliest grandpa, it could still work. "The only thing is, what would you guys want from him?"

"Maybe they're nice bad guys," Joe said. "Maybe they want to say how sorry they are."

I raised an eyebrow. Not the direction I'd been going in my head, but it was an interesting approach. One that would maybe throw Dylan off guard.

"Okay. But I don't know if Ignacius is in. Besides, Ian has this information. He'll probably talk to Dylan himself."

"Perhaps so, but his response to a detective will be different than two of Big Jimmy's men." Pavani sipped her tea.

It was worth a shot. I glanced at Joe. "Would you want to do this?"

"If it helps."

"Are you a good actor?"

"Of course. Look at me," he said, "I was born to act." He pretended to flip back long hair he didn't have.

I giggled.

"Ignacius not so much," Marilyn said. "He'll need coaching."

"And you're really okay with us doing this?"

Marilyn shrugged. "Why not? You're not hurting anyone. If anything, you're wasting your own time. Best case scenario, you actually give Ian something worth investigating. It would be incredible if we actually solved this case." She smiled to herself.

Why did I get the feeling she didn't care so much about solving the case for her career, but rather for the purpose of impressing a certain detective?

And why did that bother me?

If anything, all of this would make the neighbourhood watch feel like they were doing something useful and there really was no harm in talking to people in public.

"Right now, who are our main suspects?" I asked.

Everyone perked up at this and Joe took out his notebook. He flipped to the right page and glanced at the bar where Pearl was handing out drinks to two middle-aged men.

"Well, Pearl because she knew about the affair and was the only obvious person to benefit from Harriet's death," he said.

I narrowed my eyes. "Why was Harriet researching poisonous plants?"

"Do you think she was up to something bad?" Joe asked.

"Nathan was never going to dump Pearl. Otherwise he would have done that already. What if Harriet finally started to realise that."

"So she wanted to kill Nathan?" Marilyn asked.

"No, she might have wanted to get rid of Pearl. She was still helping Nathan out with his debt. She wouldn't have done that if she had been planning on killing him."

"Do you really think Harriet would do something like that? What if it was her boyfriend who researched those plants?" Pavani asked.

"He said he was going to break up with her, so why would he? Unless he was lying, of course. Anyone can be lying, even Pearl."

We all watched her while she laughed at something Agnes said.

"Harriet had been talking to Dan a lot, and even though Ian spoke to him, I think it might be different if I talk to him. I'm working there tomorrow anyway, so I might as well fish for info." I took a sip of my drink, already contemplating what I'd say.

"We also need to remember the killer typed a goodbye letter," Joe said. "They weren't planning on Harriet being found."

"Which means we should also talk to the boyfriend," Pavani said. "Find out who had access to their home and computer."

"Yes, good point."

"Perhaps I can talk to the boyfriend," Pavani said. "I will simply be a caring neighbour. I'll bring some cake over. People find it easy to talk to me."

"That's a good idea."

"And then when will Ignacius and I talk to Dylan?" Joe asked. He seemed excited about it already, despite his earlier hesitation.

"Actually, I think we'll let Pavani talk to him first. Maybe she can get him to talk about Big Jimmy." I smiled at her.

She beamed back. "Thank you. I think I can do that."

Ian entered the pub and the smile that was about to pop up on my face froze. His posture screamed he was in detective mode. His eyes immediately went to the bar. Or rather, Pearl. I held my breath as I saw him walk over with a frown.

Pearl greeted him with a laugh and a greeting I couldn't make out. He leaned forward and told her something that made her go pale. She stared at him while he glanced around the pub and then beckoned her with a nod of his head. She took off her apron and went over to Agnes who was carrying two plates on a tray. Her cheerful expression also fell as she listened to whatever Pearl had to see and then glanced at Ian. She was about to say something when Pearl followed Ian out of the pub. Agnes stood there, frozen, watching them go.

Something was very wrong.

"What's that all about?" Joe asked, having followed it as well.

I got up and rushed out of the pub, just in time to see Pearl get into a police car. Someone bumped into me and I was sure it was Joe.

"Pearl just got arrested," I said.

Betty bleated next to me, causing me to jump. Whatever she was saying in sheep language, I agreed.

Chapter Twenty-Seven
A Beneficial Friendship

BOTH PAVANI AND I HELPED out Agnes with orders. It was getting busier by the second and I wasn't sure if it was because of what happened with Pearl or just because it was getting close to dinner time.

At least this kept me from worrying. Still, I couldn't help but contemplate what it was that had made Ian bring Pearl in. Was there new evidence? If so, why had they only found it now? And what could it be? And what about Nathan? Was he going to help her out or drop her like a hot potato? Could she have really killed Harriet?

Not long after, it was gossip galore and when it finally quieted down enough for me to join the neighbourhood watch—which was now complete—I had heard very disturbing things.

I sat down in the booth. Agnes remained on her feet as usual. There were about fifteen people in the pub, but she wouldn't sit down in case someone wanted something. It was ten PM. One more hour till closing.

Ignacius was sipping tea. It was a fresh pot that Agnes had just put down. Pavani poured for me when I grabbed an empty cup from the tray.

"What have you heard?" Joe asked. "Because from this table I only managed to catch something about someone's hemorrhoids."

I made a face.

"I heard someone overheard a shouting match between Pearl and Harriet," Pavani said.

"I heard someone saw Pearl drive Harriet's car," Marilyn added.

"And I heard someone saw them argue." Agnes's brows were drawn together as she said this.

I groaned and they all looked at me. "I heard that someone actually saw Pearl strangle Harriet."

They were quiet as they processed this.

"I guess that's it. Mystery solved." My voice was monotone. I felt like I had lost something, but I wasn't sure what. Perhaps I was just frustrated about believing Pearl and being wrong.

"If you guys don't mind, I think I'm just going to bed early." I got up.

"I'm sure Ian will come for a last drink. He can fill us in. Maybe she wasn't arrested, maybe they were just discussing a new clue," Agnes said. The look in her eyes wasn't one of panic, but she was clearly also upset. Why wouldn't she be? She had been working with Pearl, albeit briefly.

"I'll hear it all tomorrow. I'm tired." I gave her a kiss on the cheek. It was an impulse. She smiled and touched my cheek.

"Goodnight, dear."

I glanced at the table of... friends? "Goodnight, guys."

They all said goodnight and flashed me smiles, despite the depressing mood in general. I sauntered back to my flat and as soon as I saw the light on in Ian's flat, I dashed into my bedroom and opened up the door to the French balcony.

He was right there, staring up at the sky, but then visibly startled by the sound I made when opening up my door.

"Hey," I said.

"Hi, you scared me." He chuckled.

"Sorry, didn't mean to. I was just surprised to see you up here. Agnes was convinced you were going to show up at the pub soon."

He winced. "Yeah, I figured she would be. The thing is, I just wanted some time to myself, think about the case."

"So, it's not over?"

He glanced down into the narrow alley between us. "It's not really handy to talk about it here, like this."

"You're right. I have booze." I raised an eyebrow at him.

He smiled. "I'll be right over."

A brief moment later we were in my living room where I poured him a Jack Daniels. I had one as well. We were past wine at this point.

His arm rested on the back of the sofa and I had pulled up one knee. It was nearly touching his thigh.

"So, did she really do it? You can say that much, can't you?" I asked.

"We don't know if she did it." He took a sip of his drink and closed his eyes for a second, as if to savour the taste.

"So what made you bring her in?"

He looked at me. "We got an anonymous tip from a witness who claims he or she saw Pearl fight with Harriet."

"He or she? You don't know the voice?"

"No. They sounded muffled according to my colleague. We questioned Pearl as long as we could, but without an actual witness who wants to come forward, we've still got nothing."

I nodded. "Kind of interesting that this witness came forward all of a sudden."

"Yes, I thought that as well. It could be that someone is getting nervous and wants to frame Pearl, but it could also simply be that it is the truth and they have finally summoned the courage to call it in," Ian said. "It happens."

"I see." I took a sip of my drink. "What do you think?"

"About Pearl killing Harriet? It's possible. She certainly had a motive. It wouldn't surprise me if this was all about Nathan. Harriet was willing to do a lot for him."

"Right. But I don't think Nathan would have ever left Pearl. I do believe, even though he's a total ass, that he loves her in his own way."

"But Pearl may not have known that. Perhaps Harriet said something to her during that argument that made her snap and strangle her."

"Yeah," I said, with reluctance. It made sense. I just didn't want to believe it.

"I do reckon it's a good idea to stop working there."

I bit my lip as I contemplated this. She was definitely lonely and I suppose I felt for her. But the fact that Nathan seemed to be the only thing she wanted made her a good suspect in Harriet's death. Provided that she had been a real threat to Pearl. Pearl seemed to think not when I spoke to her, but that could have been a lie.

"I'll consider it," I said.

A frown formed on Ian's face. "What's there to consider? Don't you have other clients now?"

"I do, but I feel kind of bad for Pearl. I mean, if she is indeed innocent. And like you said, you just don't know if she did it."

He leaned forward. "Which means she also *could* have done it. Why would you take the chance?"

I shrugged.

"Don't you care?"

"Not really."

"You don't care what happens to you?" He put down his drink.

I shrugged again. "Not really."

"I don't like that."

"Why not?"

We stared at each other.

Don't do it. Don't do it. Don't do it, I told myself.

He reached out to touch a strand of my hair, and it was enough to push me over the edge. I grabbed his collar and kissed him.

He froze in surprise for a brief moment, but then his hand that had reached for my hair cupped my face. His thumb stroked my cheek and his lips felt soft and warm.

I wanted to stay in this moment forever, but I knew I couldn't. Still, I scooted closer to him, deepening the kiss. His hand moved to the back of my neck and he let his fingers slide through my hair.

My lips were buzzing and my whole body was tingling. We kissed for a while but finally Ian broke away. He looked a lot sexier with his mouth swollen and his expression wild.

He cleared his throat and repositioned himself. "Wow, okay." His voice was hoarse. "I think we should take it a bit slower." He risked a glance at me. "Don't look at me like that."

"What? What look am I giving you?"

"You're smirking. It's sexy. Stop it."

I laughed. "I wasn't aware I was doing that, nor was I aware that me smirking was sexy."

He smiled at me. "Well, it is." His smile fell. "Look, I do want to take things slower. I really—I really like you. I don't want anything to go wrong."

My stomach dropped. Of course things would go wrong. And how could I do that to him? This had been a terrible mistake. Every interaction with him had been a mistake. I should have never let him get to me. That smile, his smell, everything else that I liked about him. I couldn't help that I liked those things, but I could have chosen my responses.

What was it my mother had said? *You can't control your feelings, but you can make someone think you can.*

"You make it sound as if you want a relationship," I said, managing to keep my voice level. I had to come off cool and collected.

He frowned at me. "Don't you?"

Ian had been ready for a family, he had been looking to settle down and his wife had pretended to want those things but then turned around and hurt him. She'd called him boring.

"I don't really do relationships. They're boring."

His frown deepened and his mouth opened as if he wanted to say something but wasn't sure what.

"Can't we be friends with benefits? Keep things casual." I knew he'd say no.

He looked down at his hands but still didn't say anything.

Was he seriously considering it? Or was he just contemplating how to let me down?

"I'll think about it," he finally said.

"What?"

He looked up at me. "Yeah. I'll think about it. I've never done anything like that, but let me consider it."

He liked me that much? No, that was ... perfect, actually. If we could keep things casual then it would be easier in the end. Right? Right. Of course.

"I should go now. I'm tired. I'll quickly go down and say bye to Agnes." He got up.

I got up as well and walked him to the door. "I had fun. Bye."

His smile was charming as always. "Me too." He leaned forward and kissed my cheek.

After he was gone, I rested my forehead against the door. My feelings felt all tangled up, and I wasn't sure how to untangle them. But I had to help my mother and I had only just gotten here. I couldn't give up now.

Chapter Twenty-Eight
Wise Words

THE NEXT MORNING, I was up bright and early. Ian's blinds were still closed and even Agnes wasn't downstairs in her kitchen. Betty was in the back garden so at least she couldn't cause any trouble.

My first stop was Nathan's. I knew it was risky, but I wanted to see how Pearl was doing. I left a note downstairs for Agnes so that she knew where I was, just in case something went wrong.

It would be quite inconvenient if I got murdered.

When I arrived at the Georgian estate, only Pearl's car was in the driveway. It was possible she was out on a run or something, but I had the feeling she'd be home. She was probably shaken by yesterday.

I let myself in and checked the chart so I could see what needed doing. I decided to just work as usual today and make my decision after. To be fair, I didn't need this job anymore, but there was something vulnerable about Pearl. My mother would be disappointed in my empathy.

I got out the Dyson and froze when I realised someone was watching me. I slowly turned around to Pearl in her pyjamas. She stood on the staircase, her eyes widened.

"You came," she said to me.

"I did. It's Monday."

"But you came. I mean, didn't you see Ian take me in for questioning? Why are you here?" She went down the stairs and stood in front of me.

I shrugged. "You still need a maid, don't you?"

She hugged me.

It was so unexpected, I nearly dropped the hoover. "Are you okay?"

"No, I'm not okay. I mean, I am," she said as she let go. "But also, I'm not. The police seem to really think I did it, but I didn't. And to make matters worse, Nathan has gone off to find me a good lawyer. He's going to beg his dad for help, but I doubt he'll lift a finger for me. He thinks I'm trash."

"I'm glad Nathan is doing his best to help you," I managed to say. Credit where credit's due.

"I bet the whole village is in an uproar. I'm surprised nobody has showed up with torches. There was apparently a witness who claimed they saw something, but I never met Harriet outside of work. It makes no sense." Pearl teared up. "All this time I thought she was pranking us for attention, then she turned up dead. And now, to make matters even worse, people think I did it."

"You said she'd been avoiding you, but you must have realised that it was because of the affair once you hired that private investigator."

Pearl nodded. "Yeah, I realised. I figured she felt guilty. But when there was that blood in that bathroom, I thought maybe Nathan had ended things and she wanted his attention."

"Right. And before that she had never dropped hints about the affair, or tried to confront you about it in any way?" I asked.

"No. Why?"

"I'm just trying to figure out what her state of mind was before she got killed. See, I think she was working on getting Nathan to choose her and I think he was happy enough to continue using her. But something must have happened. Something that led to her death. I am missing something, but I feel like I'm close to understanding it, if that makes sense. I'm sorry if I'm confusing you."

Pearl shook her head. "No, I'm glad you are confiding in me. It means that at least two people believe in me." She clasped my hands. "I'm so thankful I met you. I mean that, Clara."

I muttered a few incoherent words as I blushed. People never really complimented me like that. But to be fair, I hadn't been so involved with people before. Even with cons I had always kept my guard up and did whatever my mum told me. But this, this was different.

"I'll go and clean now." I let go of her hands.

"Yeah, of course." She cleared her throat. "Agnes asked me to come in tonight, said I was welcome to work as long as I want to, but I'm not sure if it's a good idea." She raised her eyebrow and looked at me, as if awaiting my advice.

I shrugged. "Do whatever you want. Who cares about what strangers think? Also, what are they going to do? Not give you their orders?"

Pearl blinked. "Right. Right. You are absolutely right. I will go. Because I want to. And nobody is going to stop me." She smiled and shook her phone at me. "I'll go give her a ring right now. What would I do without you?"

I returned her smile. She would find out one day. Hopefully soon. The sooner I could help my mother, the better.

While she went into the other room, I started cleaning. I had put in earphones and music. Pearl wasn't my only client today.

WHEN I ARRIVED AT REGINALD'S it was quiet. His daughter let me in and then went off to go horse riding with friends. I had the feeling it was a euphemism for drinking wine and talking about men.

Reginald was sitting in the dining room. The table was large and narrow and he was staring at a photo album.

"Hey, Reginald." I sat down next to him, holding my cleaning caddy. I set it down on the floor. "How are you doing?"

He looked up and winked at me. "Still pretending to have one foot in the grave."

"What are you looking at?"

He sighed as if everything was tough for him today. "Just looking at memories, I suppose. Time has flown by so quickly. It's so strange. One day you're a young lad in your twenties, and the next moment you're an old widower."

"I'm sorry," I said, unsure of what else I could say.

"Don't be. It beats dying young." He turned to me. "How are you?"

I blinked at him. He asked as if he really cared. As if a single 'okay' wouldn't be enough to satisfy him. He wanted a real answer.

Due to my upbringing I'd always considered myself guarded, and yes, I'd only really had casual friendships after I left the family business, so to speak. But that was also because I never went out and *tried*. Perhaps because I was scared. And ever since I got here, these people have been open and warm. They immediately made me feel like it was safe to be myself, and I needed that so much.

As long as I didn't tell them of my plans, it was probably safe to lower my guard a little.

"I'm not sure." I frowned. "I guess there are several things weighing on me."

He nodded, but didn't say anything.

I bit my lip and looked at my hands. "The first thing is Harriet's murder. I feel invested, though I'm not sure why. I thought it was to impress the neighbourhood watch, and perhaps that's how it started, but I think it has grown into an opportunity for me to use my skills for good. I feel like I'm valuable and I like that."

"That makes sense. We all want to do something meaningful with our lives."

I raised an eyebrow as I thought of my mother. She definitely didn't want to do anything meaningful. She just wanted to make and spend lots of money. But I had always known I wasn't like her.

"I want to look into it, but at the same time I feel like it's not my place," I said.

"As long as you're just asking a few questions, what's the harm?" Reginald asked. "You should always trust your instincts. As long as you are careful, you really have nothing to lose."

"I suppose so." I wasn't sure if I could actually figure out who the killer was, but perhaps I could provide a clue that would make Ian crack the case.

"When I was a young lad," he started, and leaned forward, "a long, long time ago," after which he leaned back again, "I witnessed a fight. I say fight, but it was really more of a beating. It was three boys against one. His name was Norman and he was regularly ridiculed because he had an interest in insects."

"Insects?"

"Yes. He later became an entomologist. Anyway, I saw it happen and I stood frozen for a few seconds, before finally getting a teacher. By then, the boys had already left and I felt incredibly dismayed. Norman refused to tell the teacher who beat him up and when I later asked him about it, he said it was because they were going to continue doing it anyway."

Reginald shook his head at the memory.

I couldn't blame him. I was getting angry just listening to it.

"The thing was, I just couldn't stand something so unfair happening. So I devised a plan. I was going to be Norman's bodyguard without him even knowing. We weren't friends or anything, so instead of walking with him, I just followed him around each day after school. Of course it wasn't long before these boys cornered him again."

I nodded, eager to learn what his plan had been.

"I got out my slingshot and started shooting at them while I acted possessed. I started hollering and shrieking and dancing as if I had ants in my pants."

A laugh escaped my lips. I clamped my hand over my mouth.

"No, no, it is funny. They ran off. So, it worked. And Norman and I actually became friends for a while. My point is, I understand the feeling of wanting to do something. Especially since it happened to a woman who was working with you."

"Yeah," I said. "I think it's just that this village feels so wonderful and connected, and this murder just taints that. I want the person responsible to be locked up and for everyone here to be safe again."

"You're a good person," he said with a smile.

I pressed my lips together. "No, you're a good person."

He laughed. "If only my daughter noticed."

Right. It was beyond me how his daughter could be so different from him. Then again, I was also vastly different from my mother. Parents may teach their kids a lot, but values can still differ.

"And what's the second thing?"

I blinked at him. "Oh, right. I'm not planning on staying here long."

Reginald just regarded me with patience, sensing there was more to that. Perhaps there was a reason we had met.

"I think I might be in love," I blurted out and consequently felt my cheeks burn.

"Congratulations," he said.

"Congratulations?"

"Love is always something that should be celebrated. Even when you know it will end." He touched his wedding ring.

I swallowed. "It doesn't feel like cause for a celebration."

"That's because you're focussing on the end. Everyone and everything has an end. But focussing on only that will just be depressing. You never know what beautiful things you will encounter along the way, so just enjoy the ride."

I hadn't realised my shoulders were tense until I leaned back in the chair. "That's actually very wise."

He nodded. "With age comes wisdom and since I'm very old, I'm very wise."

I chuckled. "I don't even need to make old age jokes, you make them for me."

"See? Part of my wisdom." He winked at me.

Reginald was seriously growing on me.

"Thanks, Reginald."

"If I may ask. Why are you planning on leaving?"

"My mother."

He leaned forward with a conspiratorial smile. "The spy."

"Exactly," I said, trying to match his grin. "She's sick and she needs me. I'm trying to make as much money as I can before returning to her."

His grin vanished. "I'm sorry. I completely understand."

"Thanks. I appreciate that."

"You know, don't be afraid to lean on some of the people here. They can be lovely. Even my daughter might surprise you. She knows loss."

"Yeah, I'm sorry. It must have been rough on her."

"It was like a switch had been flipped. She was too afraid to care or to love. And she started focussing on things that would never leave her. Things that could be touched. Shallow things. Emotions were too risky."

I felt a pang of recognition at that last bit. It was very likely that my mother focussed on shallow things because she was afraid of love as well.

It also made me understand Florence more.

"It makes sense," I said. "But it also means that when you lost your wife, you lost a big part of your daughter. I'm so sorry."

Sadness flashed in his eyes. "Let's not be too depressing. There's plenty to be thankful for."

I nodded. Wow, he was very strong. I wondered if there was something I could do to bring Florence and him closer. Probably not. I wasn't a psychologist, I was just their maid.

Even if it wasn't part of my job, I made Reginald a cup of tea and a sandwich and parked him in front of the TV before I started cleaning. When I was done, Reginald was snoring on the sofa. I put his plate and mug away and stepped outside.

Dan was sweeping the area in front of the stables. This time it was cloudy and he had a shirt on. This would be a good time to ask him some questions.

Chapter Twenty-Nine
Putting the Pieces Together

"HEY, DAVE, IS IT?" I asked him as I approached him. I wanted to throw him off balance.

He stared at me for a few seconds as if he couldn't quite believe I hadn't remembered his name. "It's Dan, actually." He flashed me a charming smile.

"Ah, Dan. I'm terrible with names. And faces."

"We all have our strengths and weaknesses," he said.

"I've been meaning to tell you...I'm sorry about Harriet."

He stopped sweeping and ran a hand through his hair. "Why are you telling me this?"

"She mentioned you."

He frowned. "She did?"

"She didn't mention your name, but she said she had a friend at Reginald's."

The corner of his lips turned downwards. "Yeah. I guess we were kind of friends. I keep telling myself I shouldn't be upset because it's not like we hang out after work, but we did spend a lot of our breaks together."

"You have the right to be upset," I said.

He nodded. "I guess so."

"Did you hear how Pearl got brought in for questioning?"

"Of course. Who hasn't?" He put down the broom and gestured at a wooden bench on the other side of the stable.

"Does it surprise you?" I asked as I followed him. We sat down.

"Yes and no," he replied. "Yes, because, well, who would kill someone like that? And no, because—" his voice trailed off and he looked at me. "How much do you know?"

He wanted to know if I knew about the affair. "I know about Nathan."

"Right. Well, the whole Nathan thing was a mess."

"Why do you say that?"

"Because she was obsessed with him even though she already had a boyfriend."

"Yes. I got that impression."

"But it's also why I can picture Pearl and Harriet fighting and it ending ugly."

"Do you think that's what happened?"

"The last time I spoke to Harriet she was moody. She was thinking of giving Nathan an ultimatum and when I asked her what she'd do if he wouldn't break it off with Pearl, she acted as if that wouldn't be a problem, as if she had some kind of plan. To be honest, when I heard she was gone, I just figured he hadn't picked her and she'd run away for a fresh start. She never liked cleaning anyway. I think she was more interested in Nathan's wealth than anything else."

"You figured she just couldn't handle not getting her way," I said.

"Exactly." He looked at the ground. "But then she was found dead in the boot of her car. Sickening."

"Agreed." I thought of something. "I know the detective came and asked you about Harriet. Why didn't you tell him this?"

"I had just heard she'd died. I didn't want to say anything that made her look bad. Besides, it's not like anyone else had gotten hurt, so I figured it was not worth mentioning."

Dan didn't have a reason to lie, and it made sense. It would explain why she had looked up poisonous plants. She wanted to get rid of Pearl. But how would she ensure that any poison would be ingested by her? And not also by Nathan? It was possible she knew what kind of stuff she drank that Nathan didn't, but even so, would she risk hurting Nathan?

I had to consider what I did know. She was put in her car and the car was pushed into the lake near Nathan and Pearl's house. It meant she had driven somewhere, right? Maybe she met up with Pearl for a walk or something? Maybe she wasn't just dumped in the woods, but maybe that's where it happened.

Too much speculation. But I wanted to run with the idea because she would have been too eager not to make a move. If they had met, Pearl and Harriet would have definitely fought because Pearl already knew about the affair. So perhaps the fight truly was witnessed by someone and it would mean she's the killer.

I needed to talk to Pearl. But I wouldn't go alone.

"THIS IS QUITE EXCITING," Ignacius said as he touched his collar.

"Is it?" I asked. We were waiting on a dirt path in the woods near Nathan's. Since Nathan was home, this is where we'd agreed to meet with Pearl. She knew I'd brought the vicar and she knew what we wanted to talk about. I figured bringing Ignacius was the safest bet. He was kind and I hoped he'd help lower her guard.

"I'm rather nervous," he said.

"Don't be. Our goal is to make her feel like she can tell us anything and that we're on her side."

I got out my phone to record the conversation.

"But we're not, right?"

"No. I'll text Ian if she does confess, though hopefully we can convince her to turn herself in."

"Got it. Don't worry. I'm excellent at putting people at ease. People tell me their whole life stories all the time. I know a lot of things." He frowned. "A lot of disturbing things."

I raised an eyebrow. From the corner of my eye I caught movement. "Oh, here she comes."

Pearl was wearing jeans and a white cardigan that looked expensive. She wasn't wearing much jewellery and had on a lot of makeup. She looked as glamorous as ever.

"Hi, guys," she said. Her voice contained tension. She was nervous.

"Hello," I said. "Did you ever formally meet Ignacius?"

"Err, yes, in the pub. I think Agnes introduced us."

"Indeed she did. Lovely to see you again, dear." He shook her hand.

"So, what's this about then? Did you hear more rumours? Is a mob out to get me?" Pearl asked me.

"Let's take a walk," I said.

"Okay." We started heading down the dirt path, deeper into the woods. The sun was shining and birds were chirping. A very cheerful setting for a not-so-cheerful topic.

Pearl walked in-between us.

"We want to help you," I said. "Which is why we've done some digging. And it seems like Harriet wanted to hurt you."

"What do you mean?" She looked up at me, question marks in her eyes.

I figured she was going to lie. "I mean, she'd been researching poisonous plants and was planning on using them."

She stopped in her tracks and grabbed my arm. "Excuse me? Are you saying she was going to *kill* me?"

Ignacius moved over to my side. "We think so, dear."

"We know so," I added. I wanted Pearl to believe we knew, beyond the shadow of a doubt.

Her makeup prevented me from seeing if she actually turned pale, but her bottom lip trembled for a moment. "How could she? Why—I mean, I know why. She wanted to be with Nathan and that's the only thing she could think of doing. Not that he'd still be with her. She was just the maid." She held up her hand at me. "I'm sorry. I didn't mean it like that."

"It's okay."

She stomped her foot and grunted with anger. "I can't believe it."

I noticed her jaw was clenched and her brow furrowed. She was angry. So perhaps that meant she didn't know Harriet had wanted to kill her. It just happened that she killed her first.

"But we also know that she was going to make her move," I said. "The night she died."

She frowned and looked from me to Ignacius and back to me again. "How do you mean?"

"Harriet wanted to kill you the night she died. So, what happened? Did she ring your doorbell? Or did she call you?" It would have shown up on her phone records but obviously Harriet would have used a different phone. Probably one of the phone booths that were in this village.

Her mouth opened and then shut again as her shoulders sagged. "You think I killed her." She didn't even phrase it as a question.

"We think you defended yourself," Ignacius said in a kind tone. "We understand why. She wanted to kill you."

I nodded. "We're here to help."

Tears welled up in her eyes.

Here we go. She was going to confess.

"How could you? I thought you believed in me!" She looked at me and let out a sob.

Wait. What?

"I thought we were friends." She wiped away her tears.

Oh, no. Why did I feel bad? "D—don't cry," I said. Was she really not guilty or was I falling for the oldest trick in the book: tears?

"Look, I didn't kill Harriet. She didn't show up at the house. I didn't kill her. Not even the detective can prove it. And you know why? Because I'm innocent."

She turned around and practically ran back towards the house.

Ignacius and I looked at each other.

"That went well," he said.

I bit my lip. "Maybe Nathan opened the door instead."

"Possibly," Ignacius said. "But again, how do we prove it? Also, if he really didn't care for her, why bother killing her?"

"This is so frustrating." I ran my hands over my face. "Do you think Pearl's lying?"

Ignacius patted me on the back. "How about we take a break? You've been working all morning and afternoon. Let's take a breather and think about this. Pub?"

"Pub."

Chapter Thirty
Target Acquired

I PARKED MY CAR IN the parking space opposite the pub.

"Don't look so sad. It will be okay," Ignacius said. "I'll treat you to a nice lunch."

I smiled. "I appreciate that. And thanks for coming along with me."

"Of course. I have to be your bodyguard." He pretended to show off his muscles.

"And you make a fine one." I chuckled.

We got out and headed to the pub. My gaze went towards the bookshop next to it. The one time I'd gone in I'd gotten distracted by Dylan. Perhaps I should have a browse to cheer me up.

"Hey, can you order something yummy for me? I just want to dash into the bookshop and have a look around. I'll be five minutes."

"Of course. Take your time. I'll order something that will bring us closer to heaven. I mean, if you believe in that sort of thing."

I bit my lip to keep from laughing. "Of course. Thanks."

The shop was quiet and I immediately zoomed towards the romance section. Perhaps I could find a good book to download for my e-reader. I picked up one of the books and smelled the pages. One thing I really missed when it came to my trusty device.

"Looking for anything in particular?" Harry had popped up next to me. His cheeks were rosy and his smile warm. He had such a nice vibe to him. He really was suitable for working in a cosy bookshop.

"I'm just getting a few ideas about books I can add to my list. I feel like reading something cheerful and romantic." I put down the book.

"An excellent choice of genre. I do like the occasional romance novel myself."

I smiled at him, then turned serious. "How's your son doing?" Had he spoken to Pavani already?

"Oh, he's keeping busy. He's in the back. I figured it would be better since he's grieving."

"Yes, probably wise. It's very sad that his romance came to an end that way." It was hardly a romance, but I was curious to see if Harry knew that Dylan was about to break up with her. I wasn't sure if he and his son were that close.

"Quite. Poor lad. He was even going to propose to her. It's just heartbreaking to think that someone would do something so incredibly evil. I hope Ian will catch the monster soon."

I nodded automatically but my mind was in hyper drive. He'd told me he was going to break up with her and had gotten upset when I mentioned she'd told me she loved him. I thought that was because he missed her, but what if it was guilt? If Pearl was telling the truth, it meant Harriet had been prevented from going over.

Dylan proposed, or maybe not even, perhaps he'd found out she was researching poison and realised she was going to kill Pearl. Meaning, she wasn't going to stay with Dylan. Either way, it would have resulted in a fight. He ended up strangling her, wrote the goodbye letter, put her in the boot of her car and drove to that lake. He would have had to walk all the way back, but it was possible.

What about the blood in the bathroom? Right. She had a key to their place. He could have taken it and sneaked in. It's a big place. He could have used a sponge or something to collect the blood from her arm.

I made eye contact with Dylan. He was by the counter and judging by his wide eyes he had overheard his dad. He knew I knew.

The bell above the door tinkled. Ian stepped inside with a coffee to go. He smiled at me and was about to say something when he paused and glanced from me to Dylan.

Dylan bolted. He flew into the back and I went right after him.

"It's him," I shouted to Ian, hoping he knew what I meant.

"What is going on?" Harry called after me.

I followed Dylan through the back. He pushed open the back door but I was right on his heels. He was quick, though. He dashed through the alley and turned the corner into the alley between the pub and the bookshop. Ian was at the end of it. He no longer had his drink in his hand.

Dylan stopped, nearly falling over as he came to a sudden halt. I stopped as well. He went for me and probably wanted to push me aside, but I ducked out of the way and then swung my right fist right into his left cheek. There was a *thump* as my fist connected. He toppled over.

Ian came running and grabbed cuffs from behind him. Did he always carry those around?

"Are you okay?"

I shook my hand. "Perfect."

"That was a nice hit." He bent down to the groaning Dylan and pushed him on his stomach so he could cuff him.

"Thanks," I said.

"Care to fill me in?"

"Oh, I think Dylan can do that. Right, Dylan?"

"That really hurt," he said, sounding like a petulant child.

"Just as bad as being strangled, do you think?" I asked and got down on his level since he was still on the ground. Ian had pulled him up to a sitting position.

Dylan started crying. "I thought she loved me. I know what she could be like, but I thought she loved me."

"But she was obsessed with Nathan. Or more accurately, his lifestyle," I said.

Harry came up behind Ian. He didn't say anything and looked pale. Dylan hadn't seen him yet.

"I saw her doing something with gloves on. Later I found out it was Wolfsbane. It's very poisonous. We got into a fight about it because she wouldn't tell me what it was for. While we were shouting, she finally told me she meant to use it to kill Pearl. She wanted her out of the way so she could be with Nathan." He looked up at me, tears streaming down his face.

"And then what?"

"You don't understand! I'd been working double shifts for six weeks so I could buy her a beautiful engagement ring and this is what she was going to do. She was willing to kill to be with him. Then she said she'd kill me too if I told anyone, and I lost it. She didn't care for me at all. I grabbed her throat and didn't let go." He started sobbing again.

His dad was behind him, crying silent tears.

"And then?" Ian asked.

"I panicked first, but then calmed myself down and realised I could frame that bastard Nathan for it. So I made cuts on her forearm and collected as much blood as I could in an empty jar. It wasn't much and wasn't easy to do." He had stopped crying now and his voice sounded more distant, colder. "I put her in the boot of the car, drove to the lake, dumped her in there. Then I walked to their house. I used Harriet's key to get in and went into one of the bathrooms. Then I headed back home. I cleaned up and I wrote that letter."

"Son, how could you?" his father finally said.

Dylan whipped his head around. "Dad. Dad, I'm sorry. I just—it just happened."

"You're under arrest," Ian said, and read him his rights. Then he looked at me and nodded.

I nodded back and liked what I saw in his eyes.

Respect.

A FEW DAYS LATER I had a quick soup as lunch in-between clients. I was alone at the table. Things were stable at the pub and Pearl had officially taken on the job. Things were over between her and Nathan, and Ignacius had found her a roommate he knew from the church. She was a middle-aged woman who needed someone new after her former roommate left for Japan.

Pearl said she'd forgiven me for suspecting her after I had explained, but she was still not her usual self around me. I figured she needed time. Especially after finally having dumped Nathan.

Ian approached my table just as I finished my tomato soup. It was nice and creamy.

"Hey," I said.

"Hi." He sat down in front of me. "Finished?"

"Yeah. I have to get to my next client. Sorry."

He smiled. "Do you have just one minute?"

"Of course." I couldn't say no to anything when he smiled at me like that.

"I just—I've been thinking about what we talked about before, and I think we should give it a go. You know, no strings attached."

I closed my eyes and smiled. He really was quite something. And it was easy to tell myself to just enjoy my time with these people. After all, doing that would also benefit my cover. However, fear was powerful. And friendships were easier than romance.

"I appreciate that, but I need you to know that I care about you. And because I care about you, I want to be friends. Nothing more. I know this may sound weird, but I think it's for the best. We enjoy each other's company, right? So let's just focus on that."

"Do you really think we can be just friends? Because I think about that kiss all the time."

Me too. "Yes, I do."

He nodded slowly as if he was still considering my words. "Alright. Friends, it is." His expression didn't give away disappointment, nor relief for that matter. But I guessed he was scared as well, and therefore maybe grateful for the exit I provided.

We smiled at each other.

Yes, this felt like the right thing to do. I wouldn't get too invested this way and it would make it slightly easier to leave when it came to that.

We chatted for a few more minutes about our day, and then I really had to leave for my newest client. Darla.

Agnes intercepted me on the way out.

"I'll see you at the neighbourhood watch meeting tonight?" she asked.

"Of course. I heard Joe wanted to play Clue with us."

Agnes giggled. "I think he has gotten a taste for solving crime."

"Haven't we all?" I had to admit, punching Dylan in the face was very satisfying and so was solving Harriet's murder.

Agnes kissed me on the cheek. "Good luck at work."

"You too!" I left the pub and got into my car. At least the added bonus to solving the murder was that the neighbourhood completely trusted me. So did Ian. Though perhaps that had nothing to do with the murder. Either way, they wouldn't find it odd if I left somewhere in the near future. In fact, they would understand why. And if they were to find out about the con after that, they would probably not believe it.

I drove off to Darla's, passing Betty who was fighting a woman for a pink bra that both of them refused to let go. I chuckled.

When I arrived at Darla's, she let me in herself. My trial period hadn't ended yet so she hadn't given me a key.

"This time you can do the study. My husband isn't home. Just make sure you don't actually move anything. I mean, if you do need to move it, just put it back where it belongs. He's a bit messy, but he assures me it's all an organised mess."

"Alright, no problem."

Her perfume was heavy and she preceded me to his office in the back of the house, next to the kitchen and conservatory. The sound of her heels receded as she went back to whatever she had been doing before.

Alright, the man's study certainly was a mess. His desk was littered with files and papers. The bookcases behind him looked disorganised and several books had been pulled out and only half put back in. There was a small coffee table and chair, but both of those had stacks of books on them that fit perfectly well in the bookcases.

I sighed.

Next to the entrance was a display case that held trophies, framed certificates and several framed pictures including pictures of him as a baby with his mother. He clearly valued memories. I started there and got out my microfibre cloths that worked amazingly well with dust. I started with the trophies and worked my way towards the pictures. I picked up each frame carefully and wiped off any dust, then I wiped the cabinet so that they'd return to a dust-free spot.

I froze when I picked up one of the last pictures. My mouth became dry as I stared at one of the men in the photo.

I had found my target.

Don't miss out!

Visit the website below and you can sign up to receive emails whenever Morgan W. Silver publishes a new book. There's no charge and no obligation.

https://books2read.com/r/B-A-KGMJ-NMWPB

BOOKS2READ

Connecting independent readers to independent writers.

Did you love *The Missing Maid*? Then you should read *Prelude to Poison*[1] by Morgan W. Silver!

[2]

Maggie happily spends time with fictional people, whether it is in her book store or behind her laptop. She's about to take a leaf out of one of her own detective books, however, when she finds a dead body. Even if the hotel she finds him in is known for being cursed, it soon becomes clear he was poisoned. The cobbled streets of Castlefield are not safe, and not just because there is an evil chicken that attacks people or because Maggie's aunt Nancy wields household objects like weapons. People are scared and they turn to Maggie for help.

---

1. https://books2read.com/u/bM9W5a

2. https://books2read.com/u/bM9W5a

Writing about mysteries is easier than solving one, Maggie finds out, especially when ghost hunters believe a ghost is haunting the hotel. With people ready to blame a ghost and few clues about a human killer, it's up to Maggie to team up with her fictional detective, as well as a very real one, and use every trick in the book to catch this clever killer.

Read more at www.authormw.com.

Also by Morgan W. Silver

Maggie's Murder Mysteries
Prelude to Poison
Poised to Quill
Booked For Murder

Maid for Murder
The Missing Maid

Monday Moody
The Chrono Unit
Unparalleled Affairs

Standalone
The Exciting Life of a Minor Character

Watch for more at www.authormw.com.

9 789083 164137